Big Trouble at Flat Rock

It was with a near-broken heart and a deep hatred that Jim McKendry looked down at his father lying dead in his coffin.

He could barely look at the lifeless face and the silk wrapping that covered the ghastly wound across his father's throat.

Jim swore that someone would pay for his father's death and no matter what it took the killer would be brought to justice – alive or dead.

Big Trouble at Flat Rock

Elliot Long

A Black Horse Western

ROBERT HALE · LONDON

Elliot Long 2010
First published in Great Britain 2010

ISBN 978-0-7090-8920-9

Robert Hale Limited
Clerkenwell House
Clerkenwell Green
London EC1R 0HT

www.halebooks.com

Typeset by
Derek Doyle & Associates, Shaw Heath
Printed and bound in Great Britain by
CPI Antony Rowe, Chippenham and Eastbourne

For Jenny Edgar and Pete Revell

CHAPTER ONE

The candle van Otis lit while he waited cast weak yellow light on the bedroom walls. It also showed amber on the folds of the drawn curtains at the window and the pieces of furniture that were distributed around the room.

When rancher John McKendry finally woke up he quickly became aware of the light and that there was somebody else in the bedroom. Van Otis had already anticipated what would happen next.

With a clear gasp of anxiety McKendry leaned over and reached for the Colt he had laid on the bedside cupboard before settling down to sleep. But, of course, it wasn't there and van Otis thought, who but a fool would have left it there? Certainly not he; as soon as he entered the room fifteen minutes ago he had removed it.

'Is this the gun you are looking for, John?' he said. He held up the rancher's Colt .45 with a long-fingered bony left hand.

McKendry sat up, his grey stare now wary, if a little

puzzled. He said, 'Just who the hell are you, mister?'

Van Otis smiled. 'Why, the man paid to kill you, John.'

McKendry was moving, but swift as a rattler strike van Otis dropped the Colt on to the bed and slipped out the slim gutting knife that was concealed in his left sleeve. One stroke, he sliced through McKendry's throat, ear to ear as he came towards him, fist clenched.

The rancher stared, transfixed for a moment. Severed arteries were already jetting blood across the room. It was splattering red against the flower-patterned wallpaper on the wall behind the bed; it was spraying crimson against the equally gaudy paper covering the opposite wall. The wall with the window in it, from which a man could look out over Flat Rock's Main Street, was also quickly daubed with scarlet. The flyspecked ceiling did not escape; blood sprinkled a string of ruby beads across the white-painted boards. Soon the beads of blood were dripping down on to the bed, the polished board floor and the other furniture in the room.

Van Otis stepped back quickly to try and avoid the worst of the sprays of blood he knew would come. Some of the blood did splatter on to his sleeve and up his suit front, but, as always, he could live with that.

The job was done.

He continued to smile his death's-head smile as he watched McKendry die. Van Otis admitted to himself he truly enjoyed this part of the killing ritual. It was his drug, his motivation and his heaven. All credit due, McKendry did try to yell out and avoid the blade coming at him. But, of course, he was far too late.

Van Otis gazed into the cattleman's startled eyes. The two orbs were staring back at him. They had the appearance of two large, petrified blisters. And as well as horror, there was a hint of disbelief in that stare, giving the impression the man was acutely regretting leaving this life.

Then blood began rolling out of McKendry's mouth and down his chin. Van Otis saw his lips were still working, as if he was desperately trying to say something; however, what sound did escape came out only as a strangled gargle. Then, seconds later, the rancher keeled over on to his right side, flopped like a banked fish for moments and then died.

Van Otis wiped his slim, razor-keen gutting blade clean, using the bits of bed linen that weren't soaked with McKendry's blood. Then he slipped the steel back into the sheath strapped to the underside of his left arm and secured the handle with the press-studs set into the flaps of leather.

After that, van Otis blew out the candle and paced to the thin faded blue curtains that were drawn across the window. He parted them and looked down on to the deserted Main Street of Flat Rock. It was dark down there, lit only by the pools of yellow light cast by the occasional coal oil lamps which were strung out along the street, swinging wildly in the ever-increasing wind.

Far as he could make out not a soul was using

those boardwalks and the noise of the gale that was now roaring in off the pitch-dark range beyond the silent town was now like a demented banshee. Dust, paper and other trash was running before it in a whirling frenzy. In addition, the gusts were causing the sash window he was looking out of to rattle alarmingly.

Now, half-blinding him, came the lightning flashes. Harsh light that bathed the false-fronted buildings opposite, silhouetting their gaunt shapes against the ebony infinity above before stark blackness once again closed down over the town. Seconds later the thunder raged like the roar of cannon across the inky vault. It shook the earth and the very fabric of the boarding house he was standing in. Van Otis held few doubts that this was not a night to be riding out in, but ride out in it he must.

He went to the door now and listened, hardly breathing. It was as silent as a tomb out there on the landing. He opened the door cautiously and looked up and then down its length. There was nothing to trouble him out there, he decided, judging from what he could see in the yellow light of the one lamp sitting in the bracket on the wall, placed midway between the landing ends.

Though this was not the most handsome building he had ever been in, he did concede it was above average for a modest range town like Flat Rock. And, as if knowing it, the black board atop of it announced its name proudly: High Life Hotel, Flat Rock's Premier Rooming House, Gaming Parlour and

Saloon. Along the bottom was scribed: *Fine Foods Served All Day.*

Van Otis smiled his tolerant death's-head smile. OK, but compared with some of the establishments he'd stayed in, like in New Orleans, San Francisco, Philadelphia and St Louis, this one came way down the list. Even so, folks around here did think it had a kind of flamboyance, was the cream of the crop. But that was the trouble with living at the ass end of nowhere.

Van Otis stepped out on to the landing. He closed the door softly behind him and cat-footed down the long corridor. At its end he opened the door that led out on to a small wooden platform with stairs running down from it into the alley.

He stepped out.

Instantly, the wind grabbed his trousers and slapped the expensive material against his long, thin legs. It also tore at his black, low-crowned, wide-brimmed hat, threatening to whip it off his head at any moment.

With impatience he searched for and found the black bandana, which he had stuffed into his coat pocket earlier, anticipating such a possibility, and wrapped it around the hat and tied it under his chin. Now he stared down the wooden stairs, the same steps he climbed to get into the building.

Before he descended he scanned the narrow alley below, which was faintly lit by a coal oil lamp swinging wildly in the wind on a hook fastened to the corner of the hotel, the front of which faced on to

11

Main Street twenty yards up. Everywhere, as far as he could make out, was free of human movement, as it should be at two o'clock in the morning in this sleepy range town where, he decided, very little of any moment happened, until now, that is.

When he was satisfied he would be unobserved he closed the door quietly behind him and walked unhurriedly down the stairs.

His gelded roan was tethered a good fifty yards up the alley. When he reached it the rain began slanting down out of the black night, exploding fountains of dust off this drab back street. Though he had anticipated it, he silently cursed the downpour as he worried his long brown saddle slicker out of his saddlebag, pulled it on and buttoned it up.

After a further look around, that still found the night was void of activity, he climbed up into the saddle. Holding his hat – the black brim of which continued to flap wildly in the wind – he turned the roan north, bowing his head against the rain that was now driving like steel rods out of the darkness. But despite the violence of the storm and his initial reaction to it, he felt warm and content inside. It had been a good night's work. All that remained now was to pick up the rest of his fee of one thousand dollars, five hundred on account, five hundred when the job was done, and he would be on his way. And even though the fee would not go to him, it was a pretty good payday for what was no more than a minute or two's work – though much planning had gone into it first off. However, as the old saying goes, if you wanted the best you had to pay for it. And, of course, Christian van Otis was the best of the best. Of that he had no doubt.

He spurred his horse and the raging night swallowed him up.

CHAPTER TWO

Nine thirty next morning, a morning that dawned bright, calm and sunlit, the girl that did the cleaning upstairs in the High Life Hotel found John McKendry's blood-soaked body sprawled on the equally blood-soaked bed. In her terror and shock she dropped everything. Her shaking hand went to her mouth. Then she screamed long and shrilly before falling to the floor in a swoon.

Twenty minutes later, after inspecting the carnage, Marshal Larson Rigby looked at his deputy, Malcolm Delaney, and said, 'By God, Mal, in twenty years of keeping the peace in this town I've never seen the like of it.'

'Nor me,' Mal Delaney said.

Rigby turned to Jedidiah Bartlow, the town's carpenter and undertaker. Jedidiah was standing silent and solemn-faced close by. Rigby said, with a great sigh of genuine regret, 'Well, you'd better take him down, Jed.'

Bartlow nodded and waved a hand to the two men

behind him. 'OK, boys,' he said, 'you heard the marshal.'

The men were permanent barflies he hired ten minutes ago in the Saddleman's Rest at the north end of town – a dollar to be split between the two of them when the job was done.

Though John McKendry was not all that big, he was large enough to cause the men to grunt as they lifted him and carried him along the landing and down the rear stairway to the back alley. At the bottom of the stairs they picked their way through the ankle-deep mud, left after last night's storm, to Jedidiah Bartlow's office and workshop, the office part of which faced on to Flat Rock's Main Street. Jedidiah, as was usual on occasions like this, was clad in black from head to toe. He followed closely behind the two barflies, his hands clasped together and resting on his lap, his head bowed as if in pious contemplation of this recent tragic event.

When they got to the workshop door facing on to the side street Jedidiah called a halt. He unlocked the door and said, 'Better take him in this way, boys, we don't want Mrs McKendry and Betty Lou to see poor John until I've cleaned him up and covered that God-awful wound in his throat.' Bartlow shook his narrow head, which was perched atop of a long scrawny neck. 'By God, boys, I ask you . . . who could have done such a terrible thing?'

'Weren't human, that's for sure,' said one of the sweating body carriers, after spitting a jet of tobacco juice into the mud.

15

Bartlow nodded solemnly. 'Indeed, indeed.' The sigh that followed the words was heart-felt. By jiminy, he had known John McKendry for nigh on twenty-five years. In his opinion, no finer man ever walked this earth. This was a terrible way to go meet his maker.

Jedidiah let the barflies into the workshop and closed the door. Then he walked up the side street, squelching through the sucking mud to his office. Before he entered the premises he carefully scraped the bulk of the cloying mire off his boots on the edge of the boardwalk. Several people, he observed, were already gathered there on Main Street, in front of the office. They were apparently indifferent to the sludge they were standing in. They appeared only to want to know about the dreadful murder of John McKendry. Bartlow acknowledged in his mind that news, good or bad, travelled fast in Flat Rock, as it did in any range town. And without a doubt, word would be swiftly spreading across Wolf's Head Basin, the products from which helped sustain this modestly wealthy community. Ten seconds passed before one old-timer standing on the street pushed his chaw into his left cheek and said, 'This is a God-awful business, Jedidiah.'

Bartlow sighed again, heavily. 'Truly horrendous, Saul.' Then he waved a finger in the air above his head and stared fiercely at the assembly. His voice trembled with the emotion that was in him. 'But, my friends, the Lord will punish the perpetrator, never fear. If not in this life, then most certainly He will in the next.'

'Amen to that,' said a bonneted old woman who was staring at him with big, flat, grey eyes. She added, 'You'll surely be saying words over poor John when the burying time comes, Jedidiah?'

Bartlow looked at her gravely. 'Indeed yes, Mrs Jenson. I would fail in my duty if I did otherwise.'

That put a look of satisfaction on all faces. Long ago, everybody in town agreed there was the air of a minister about Jedidiah. And it was well known that Jedidiah's father was the pastor of the small town of Kinchella Creek in south Texas, before he had the misfortune to die from the effects of a Comanche arrow that buried itself deep in his lungs before the town beat off a dawn raid, spring of 1865. In fact, it was that tragic happening that decided Jedidiah, when he returned from the Civil War, to go north with John McKendry, when that rancher sent out the word he was gathering a herd with that very intention in mind and was recruiting.

And, true to his word, soon as John McKendry had enough men assembled he lost no time accumulating as many mavericks and half-wild cattle he could lay his hands on. Jedidiah recalled it was hard and painful work scratching and scraping through the border brasada chasing after those wild-eyed longhorns. But the fact was, after the Civil War, Texas was full of those fractious animals, the ranchers who owned them having gone to fight the Cause and never returned, their families scattered to hell and gone as well, probably a lot of them dead, too.

For sure, it still gave rise to misery in Jedidiah's

memory to recall those hard days and the heartache that went with them. And recalling them brought to mind the leaving of Kinchella Creek. Late spring it was, 1866, when John McKendry and his crew of Rebel 'go-to-hells' and the Mexican vaqueros John recruited upped sticks and pointed the herd north.

Jedidiah remembered that drive now with vivid clarity. It was long, arduous and full of hazard. However, he soon discovered John McKendry was a man with pronounced leadership abilities and a man of immense courage. Jedidiah also found McKendry was a resourceful man, patient, and with the stamina of three. Additionally, John was not above swallowing his pride if the need required him so to do. For, upon reaching Fort Laramie on the North Platte, John had to sell part of his herd to the Blue Coats in order to get enough money together to keep the drive going, the Confederate paper money he was left with at war's end being of no value.

John drove a hard bargain because he knew the Union forces badly needed the beeves to distribute to the forts along the Bozeman Road, built to protect the immigrant trains heading for the Montana gold fields.

At that time the Sioux under Red Cloud and the Northern Cheyenne under Dull Knife were making big trouble for the white intruders. Many were the times the drive had to fight off fierce attacks by both Sioux and Northern Cheyenne because John refused to hand over cattle in payment for safe passage. The only time he broke that rule was when they came across a bunch of starving Crows. He ordered ten beeves to be cut out for them. In the end it got to be that the men grew to have such respect for him that they would follow him down to the very Gates of Hell if need be. Indeed, they were stirring times.

Jedidiah faded his thoughts and from the boardwalk stared at the crowd on the street. His boots were now clean and he entered the office. He found Marshal Larson Rigby was already there, along with Deputy Malcolm Delaney. Rigby was busy comforting Sarah McKendry and Betty Lou McKendry, her daughter, with kind, softly spoken words. It figured, decided Jedidiah: the McKendrys and the Rigbys had been close friends since the early days in Kinchella Creek.

Sitting down at his desk Jedidiah came straight to the point, but with the quiet pastoral dignity he always adopted when he was in his undertaking role. He long ago found it was greatly appreciated by the citizens of Flat Rock in the sad hours of their particular mourning. Indeed, because there was no regular minister in Flat Rock, his eulogies at the graveside – which was all part of the burial package he offered – went down well with people over a wide area of Wolf's Head Basin.

He clasped his hands before him and leaned forward on the desk, his stare grey and intense. 'Sarah, Betty Lou, though it pains me greatly to say this, there are certain things I need to do before I can allow you to view John.'

He paused – this was never easy – and then

deferentially pointed to the two not very comfortable chairs placed against the street wall, by a dusty window streaked with muddy rain darts after last night's downpour. 'You can wait here, of course, and I will fix you coffee while you do. But I think it would be far better if you spent your time in the comfort of the High Life Hotel's handsome lounge while I administer to John. But, having said that, the choice will always be yours.'

Sarah McKendry bent and sobbed into her handkerchief. Betty Lou stared at him for a moment before she too lowered her gaze to begin worrying at the handkerchief in her white slim hands resting on her lap.

After moments Marshal Larson Rigby, as if to break the deadlock, cleared his throat and said, 'Sarah, Betty Lou, we have been friends a long time. Kate and I would be honoured to have you stay with us while Jedidiah does what he has to do.' Kate was Larson's wife. Rigby now looked apologetic. 'Nevertheless, I regret I won't be able to be with you. You must realize I have work to do right now. However, Kate will look after you both, I'm sure.'

Sarah McKendry looked up. Her faded grey eyes were already red-rimmed with the weeping she had done. And she had already decided it must be the Devil's own work that had brought Betty Lou and her here to Flat Rock at this early hour, to be greeted with the awful news of the death of her husband of thirty years' standing.

It had been John that had arranged their early

arrival in town, before he left the ranch yesterday afternoon to do business and play a few hands of cards into the early hours with friends. Rowdy Jones, he said, would prepare the four-seat buggy they had to drive them into town come first light. Not only to pick him up, but also to pick up the bolt the cloth that had been ordered three weeks ago at Mary Stenmayer's Gowns and Millinery on First Street. She and Betty Lou had been pestering him to take them in to pick it up for a week. Now was their chance, he said.

Sarah stared with dead eyes at the people on the street outside. Her knees felt like jelly and her body was a desert of hardly bearable misery. Poor John. Dear God, why? Why did he have to die and in such a terrible way? She wanted to burst out into torrents of tears but took hold of herself and gazed with misty eyes at Larson Rigby. What dear friends he and Kate were. She had known Kate Rigby, née Meriden, since their schooldays in Kinchella Creek. Sudden anger fired through her. Oh! What was the matter with her! One way or another sudden death had been a part of her life since God knew when! She would handle it as she had done a dozen times before, even though this was the man she had known and loved and cherished for more than thirty-five years.

Though her pain and despair was like nothing she had ever known, she set her chin and gathered her courage. She stepped forward and gently laid her right hand on the marshal's barrel chest. 'What a comfort it is to have such good friends at this terrible time.'

Rigby said, 'Sarah, I hope Kate and me have always been that and more.'

Sarah wiped her eyes and lifted her chin. She met the marshal's caring gaze. 'Indeed you have, Larson, and indeed I'm sure you will be in the years to come.'

'Bet on it,' Rigby said.

Betty Lou stayed silent, still looking down at her lap and worrying at the handkerchief in her hands.

After moments Rigby said, 'Sarah, though I don't want to bother you with a load of questions right now, I feel this is one I have to ask: have your boys, Callum and Jim, been notified?'

Sarah McKendry nodded. 'Yes, I've sent Rowdy Jones to do it. They're both on the south range, helping with the spring roundup and branding.' She sighed and dropped her shoulders. 'Oh, God, how I need those boys right now, Larson.'

Marshal Rigby comforted her by putting his right arm around her shoulders. 'Just remember, Sarah, until they arrive we are all here for you – the whole town – you know that.'

Sarah McKendry sniffed, straightened up and looked Larson right in the eye. Rigby was cheered by it. This was the Sarah McKendry he knew, third-generation frontier stock, like he and Kate; Texan born and bred. And like his, her family had fought the Comanche, fought Santa Ana to a standstill at San Jacinto, seen the birth of the Republic and lived through God knew what else before they got sick of the whole damned business after the Civil War and lit out for Montana.

Even then the battles weren't over. There were still the Sioux and Northern Cheyenne to fight, the big snows and winter freezes to contend with. It would have been enough to daunt any man, leave alone a woman. But Sarah McKendry stood firm by John's side through it all, as did all the other wives and daughters on that long trek north and after.

Rigby knew Sarah had only one big regret in life because Kate told him. It was the time when the Canadian doctor told her she could no longer bear children because of complications suffered during Betty Lou's birth. It was a bitter blow to both Sarah and John. But, as usual, they met it head on and got on with their lives, cherishing what they had. Recalling all that, Larson pressed Sarah's right shoulder gently. 'Let me get you and Betty Lou to home. Kate will be expecting you.'

Sarah said, 'Yes. God bless you, Larson.'

On the boardwalk, Deputy Delaney touched his hat brim respectfully and once more offered his condolences to Sarah and Betty Lou. Then, as prearranged with his boss, he moved off to circulate through town, hoping to find witnesses, and to glean what information might be useful to the investigation into John McKendry's awful death. But it would be like searching for a needle in a haystack, Mal decided, as he strode along the street. Larson and he had already worked out the method most likely used by that murderous butcher. It, more than likely, had been done in the early hours of the morning. The assassin must have used the back stairs of the High Life Hotel, crept down the landing, did his killing and returned the same way. After that, he rode away using last night's downpour as cover. It was already looking like it was going to be a near impossible task to find that murderous bastard. All possible tracks had been washed clean away by the storm.

Meanwhile, Jedidiah Bartlow watched the parties depart. Then he crossed the office floor and walked into his cluttered workshop at the back. The smell of wood shavings and sawdust was ambrosia to his nostrils. Carpentry was his life; the feel of timber under his gnarled hands, the hiss of the plane as it sped over the wood, the rasp of the saw. His father approved wholeheartedly of his choice of profession and set him to his apprenticeship even though he was only eleven years of age. 'It is the trade of Our Lord Jesus,' his father said joyously, 'therefore it must be right for the son of Isaiah Bartlow. The Lord's hand must have guided you.'

Fading his thoughts Jedidiah paid off the two barflies for their services and then set about preparing the body of John McKendry for viewing before burial. But, God knew, it was a terrible day. With the death of John McKendry a mighty big hole had been created in Wolf's Head Basin's pioneer community and Flat Rock in particular. It was a hole that would not be easily filled. And for sure whoever did this murderous thing must be brought to face the full rigor of the law.

CHAPTER THREE

Meanwhile, cheroot glowing nicely between thin lips, van Otis enjoyed the cool and pleasant ambience under the cottonwoods by Santee Creek, even though the river was in full spate and mud-dirty after last night's tremendous deluge. Being situated twenty miles north of Flat Rock and remote, van Otis determined weeks ago that Santee Creek was the ideal location to meet and receive instructions, and receive the initial and the concluding payment required for the elimination of the rancher John McKendry. *Elimination*, decided van Otis, because assassination had such an awful ring to it, to his sensitive ears anyway.

Van Otis felt completely relaxed. The downpour last night ended before dawn. His slicker, donned to protect him against the worst of it, was now back in his saddle-bag. The parts of his dark suit that got wet during the storm were now dry, due to a morning's ride under a hot sun. And the bloodstains that were splattered on the suit last night when the killing first took place were now barely discernible. Not that it mattered. After business was concluded here he would return at a leisurely pace to his home in Black Cherry Valley. There, his Chinaman, Lee Fong, would clean the suit in his usual efficient way. Then seclusion, relaxation and peace would ensue until the next call came. Van Otis sighed. It was the ideal life.

He dragged on his cheroot and exhaled smoke and then looked at the young man standing before him. He saw a tall, range-lean and with steel-grey eyes. However, van Otis was not at all impressed by the fellow's imposing demeanour; any man that needed to approach him to use his services seldom inspired him. In the end, most of them, in his opinion anyway, were weak specimens, unable to do their own killing. If they were not, why else would they call on him to use his abilities? Was it because they had the money to pay to have the elimination done? Or was it because of the need for discretion, due to their position in society? Or was it simply because they just did not have the guts for it? Van Otis mentally shrugged. Whatever the reason, not one of those suppositions influenced him. His opinion was and had always been that if a man needed an elimination done, he should do the deed himself. But then he smiled at this odd contradiction. It was bizarre thinking for a man who killed for the love of it and undertook his contracts with such feelings of anticipation and relish. Dammit, he would be denying himself the only real joy he had in his life!

He reached out with long, slim fingers that could have easily belonged to a woman. His black eyes were questioning behind eyelids that were narrowed to mere slits across his eyes.

This moment, he knew, could sometimes be tricky. Some men could get real uptight about paying the final instalment, demanding he lower the original requirement, even threatening to kill him if he did not agree. That was why the fasteners were off the haft of his gutting knife, ready for instant action.

'You owe me five hundred dollars,' he said.

Callum Bowden said, no hint of resentment, 'Any problems?'

'No problems.'

To van Otis's satisfaction the young man reached into his range coat and lifted out a wad of notes and passed them over. Van Otis took the money and prepared to put it into his pocket.

Callum Bowden said, 'Ain't you going to count it?'

What could have passed for a smile flickered across van Otis's excessively sallow, death's-head features. 'I don't think that will be necessary.'

Callum Bowden now stared at this tall, lean consumptive-looking man before him. A feeling, like an icy hand, clamped across his gut. Indeed, there was a chilling aura of menace about this man, the suggestion that death would be the price to pay if he was cheated in any way. He said, 'We may need you again.'

Van Otis's black eyes momentarily showed interest.

'We? What figures are we talking?'

'Maybe twice more, even three.'

Van Otis smiled. 'No problem.'

He folded the notes and pushed them into the inside pocket of his black jacket. He turned and prepared to leave, but Callum Bowden held up his left hand. 'How can you do it,' he said, 'cold-bloodedly kill for money? Ain't you got any conscience about it at all?'

Van Otis stared, his look like the flickering tongue of a rattler tasting the air for prey. Then he smiled again, though the grin could never be construed as friendly. It was more the malevolent gape of a hungry wolf, anticipating a hearty repast. 'My friend,' he said, his voice like the purr of a cougar, 'I would not exist but for you people, the people who are too yellow to do their own killing.' Continuing the sadistic smile, he touched the wide rim of his flat-crowned black Stetson, then took the half-smoked cheroot out of his thin-lipped mouth and flicked it into the stream. He said, 'You know how to contact me if you need me again.'

He turned away and climbed easily into the saddle. He gently heeled his roan around, his back as straight as a broom handle, his left hand on his left hip. Then, proud as a Spanish grandee he urged the roan into a steady canter and headed through the trees growing alongside the creek, before he eased the gelding up the shallow valley side and on to higher ground, heading north.

Callum Bowden watched him go over the rim of

the valley. He still felt intimidated by van Otis's menacing presence and snake-eyed appraisals. He spat cotton into the dust. His immediate thoughts were resentful. He glowered after van Otis. He said, in a low voice, 'Mister, I can kill as well as any man. But right now I need to call upon scum like you to do it for me. But come the day and the hour, we'll see who has the stomach for it.'

Feeling better for that, Callum climbed into the double-girth Texas saddle on his big sorrel and urged it into a canter.

CHAPTER FOUR

Heading east, Callum Bowden followed the rushing, muddy waters of Santee Creek. Three miles on he was surprised to see Rowdy Jones riding hell-for-leather towards him.

A murmur of contempt went through Callum to see the approach of Rafter M's ageing ex-wrangler. Eight years ago the horse Rowdy was attempting to tame smashed him against the corral rails and then rolled over him. The tumble left Rowdy with his right leg broken in two places and, having no doctors around at that time, it was set by one of the *vaqueros*, but it still left him with a pronounced limp. Not only that, he was left with a withered left arm he could not lift above shoulder height. But John McKendry did not pay him off. Rowdy was now the fetch-and-carry man for the Rafter M and still respected for his knowledge of horses and consulted regularly.

A lot of ranchers would have paid him off, decided

Callum. He now felt contempt for his surrogate father. If Callum Bowden had been boss of the Rafter M, which he soon would be anyway if his plans worked out, Rowdy Jones would have been long gone, for sure.

Rowdy slithered his wiry grey to a stop beside Callum. Callum knew the time to start acting had arrived. He looked at Rowdy's round, whiskered face with the flat broken nose in the centre of it. There was not the usual broad smile there. Rowdy's look was severe and grave.

'Big trouble at Flat Rock, Callum,' he said.

He was breathing hard after his long ride. He moved uneasily in the saddle then his anxious blue gaze met Callum's grey stare head on and he blurted, 'Dammit, there's no easy way to say this, Callum. Your pa's dead; throat cut from ear to ear. A God-awful sight if ever there was one, is what those who saw it are saying.'

Callum attempted to look shocked; he was slightly. Even though he already knew of Pa's death, the manner of his dying now horrified him. Throat cut from ear to ear? A bullet in the head was what he had envisaged, a clean and tidy end.

Damn you, van Otis!

'God Almighty,' he said. 'Has Marshal Rigby got anybody for it?'

Rowdy shook his head. 'Naw. And, word is, he isn't likely to either. Killer must have rode into town after midnight, done the job and rode out, leaving nary a trace of his passing. As you know it rained a bitch last

31

night, possibly wiped out any tracks there might have been. Though, in a town the size of Flat Rock – folks coming and going all the time – that wasn't likely to be any anyway.'

Callum now began to feel horribly uncomfortable as the enormity of what he had initiated began to hit him. Nevertheless, he managed to say, 'Does Jim know? And how are Ma and Betty Lou taking it? Especially Betty Lou.'

Rowdy said, 'Bad, as you'd expect. Jim is already on his way to town. He left Bat Losey in charge of the branding on Shell Creek and told me to ride to here and inform you of it. He said, seeing as you were here on the Santee, you'd be able to cut across the range through Devil's Gap to town. Save you ten miles, he reckoned.' Rowdy shook his grizzled head and said, with heavy emotion, 'By God, the whole town is mighty shook up about this, Callum. I ain't feeling too good about it, either.'

Callum stared. He was finding this act was already starting to become a strain but he would have to get used to it if he was to realize his ambitions. He steeled himself and said, 'Dammit, Rowdy, d'you think you've got a monopoly on that? This is my Pa we're talking about.'

Rowdy looked surprised. 'Never figured you to be all that close to John, I got to say. You spent most of your time arguing with him, what I know.'

'It don't say because we had disagreements I weren't close to him,' Callum said with as much resentment as he could muster. 'He reared me like I was his own, for God's sake. That's why I call him Pa.'

Rowdy raised ginger brows. 'Well, John allus did look upon you as a son I got to say. Dammit, Callum, I remember the day he dragged you out of that burning wagon when those Sioux attacked us down on the Powder. John always said he promised your pa and ma he would look after things if anything happened to them. I remember him making that very vow.' Rowdy shook his grizzled head. 'Why, I can see it now, like it was yesterday. Your pa, your ma, your brother and your two sisters burned up to a crisp, like they were, in their own wagon, only you saved. It was a terrible thing to look upon, Callum, God's truth it was.'

Callum glared ferociously across the space between Rowdy and himself. 'D'you think I want to hear it all again, you old coot, and right now, Pa dead and all?'

Rowdy looked slightly embarrassed. 'Hell, that was how it was. I didn't mean no hurt by it.'

'Well, you *did* hurt, dammit,' Callum said. He glared fiercely. 'Rowdy, you've got a big mouth. Mind it don't get you into trouble one day.'

Rowdy's look was now sulky. 'I told you I meant nothing by it.'

'All the same,' Callum said, 'just think on next time.' He tightened his lips, flapped a hand and sighed. 'Well, I guess I'd better head for town. Ma and Betty Lou must be in a bad state.'

Rowdy said, 'It can't be no other way.'

'I guess not,' Callum said. He dug heels into his

sorrel and waved a hand. '*Hasta la vista, anciano.*'

'And to you,' Rowdy said, but stared sourly after Callum. Just one arrogant jumped-up son of a bitch, was his opinion.

CHAPTER FIVE

Evening was closing in black, angry and promising more rain when Callum entered Flat Rock from the east. First place he headed for was Jedidiah Bartlow's oil-lamp-lit office. When he entered he saw Jedidiah was sitting at his desk.

The undertaker-cum-carpenter looked up from his ledger, in which he was writing. Jedidiah immediately put down his pen and got to his feet. Solemn-faced, he came round the desk and Callum took his offered hand and shook it.

'A terrible business, Callum,' Jedidiah said, 'truly terrible.' He waggled a finger in the air. 'But the Lord will punish, never fear.'

'I'm sure he will,' Callum said with as much sincerity as he could muster.

With a bow of his head Bartlow waved a deferential hand towards the door at the rear of the office. He said, 'Your Pa is out the back, Callum. I guess you'll want to see him. I've laid him out real good. Your Ma, Betty Lou and Jim have already viewed the body.'

Callum said, 'Thanks, Jedidiah.' He sighed heavily and raised dark brows. 'Well, better get it done, I guess.'

Bartlow paced across the office to the door leading to the workshop. They crossed the work place to the door of the room at the far end. Above that door were words in gold lettering: Chapel of Rest. Please Show Due Reverence.

'Weren't pretty, Callum,' Bartlow was saying over his shoulder. 'Whoever it was that cut John's throat just weren't human.'

Oh, he's human all right, thought Callum. He said, 'D'you know if Marshal Rigby's got any ideas on who done it, yet?'

Jedidiah Bartlow's faded grey eyes turned up. 'No, and my guess is he won't have, dead of night, raining like it was, nobody on the streets. Larson said it was as neat a job as he ever saw. His figuring is the killer snuck up the stairs side of the High Life, killed your Pa then snuck out the same way and rode off into the night. The rain just washed out all traces.' Bartlow paused and heaved a deep breath. 'Even so,' he went on, 'Larson remains optimistic; says there is always a chance something will turn up. But if you want my opinion, he just doesn't know where to start.' Bartlow shook his head. 'It's a damnable business, Callum, damnable. John was a fine man. He did not deserve to end up as he did. Everybody is asking the same question: why was it done? John didn't have an enemy in the world. It just don't make no sense at all.'

Callum said, 'You thought a lot of Pa, didn't you, Jedidiah?'

Bartlow's iron-grey stare was direct. 'I came up from Texas with him. I worked for him punching cows for five years when we got here. He set me up in this business at a piffling rate of interest when I said I'd like to start up on my own, doing the trade I knew best – carpentry, of course. Sure I thought a lot of him, still do and always will, by God.'

Callum nodded gravely. 'Yeah, didn't we all. Well, I reckon I'd best take a last look at him.'

Bartlow led him into the Chapel of Rest. Grey-suited John McKendry was all laid out neat and tidy in a polished pine box, padded inside with shiny white silk. A white silk scarf was arranged around John's throat, hiding the ghastly wound. Four ornamental brass handles adorned the outside of the casket. The top of the coffin lay to one side. A brass plaque was riveted to it with John's name, date of birth and date of death scribed on it.

Staring into the face of his surrogate father, a spasm of nerves raked across Callum's gut. He felt cold sweat forming on his upper lip and forehead. Pa looked as though he was sleeping. And for some absurd reason Callum now began to expect to see Pa's eyes flick open and stare at him in that cold steel way he had when dealing with trash. Then a vision began to form of Pa climbing out of the coffin, hands reaching out and preparing to strangle him. For God's sake, how could Pa *know* Callum Bowden had paid a man to have him killed? And how could a dead man climb out of his coffin to attack him, for Christ's sake?

Callum now felt sweat trickling down off his brow to start running down his face. He passed a shaking hand across his equally sweat-damp upper lip. He forced himself to stare at the silk neckerchief arranged around Pa's neck, hiding what must be the awful wound.

After moments, while he gathered himself, he said, trying to control the shake in his voice, 'You've done a real fine job, Jedidiah; real fitting for Pa.'

The undertaker bowed his head in acknowledgement. 'Thank you, Callum.' Then he sighed. 'John was a real big man, Callum, a man bred to his time. But I guess you don't need me to tell you that, John having brought you up.' Then Jedidiah stared at him more closely and added, 'Are you feeling all right, son?'

More fear raked across Callum's gut. He mopped the sweat off his brow and face and tried to find a suitable answer. In the end he said, 'Guess I *am* feeling a little groggy, Jedidiah. Picked up a fever yesterday, but it's passing.'

'Well, that's good,' Jedidiah said as if satisfied. 'You take care now. By the way, the burial will be day after tomorrow – at the ranch, around three o'clock. Word has been sent out so you won't have to bother about that. It is my belief most of Wolf's Head Basin will be out there at the Rafter M to pay their last respects.'

'I'll be mighty surprised if they're not,' Callum said. Then he added, 'D'you happen to know where

Jim, Ma and Betty Lou are right now?'

Bartlow raised his greying brows. 'I figure Jim could be at the High Life Hotel, but the marshal took your ma and Betty Lou in so they would be amongst friends at this terrible time.'

Callum nodded. 'It figures. Well, thank you, Jedidiah.'

He left the building. He could still sense Pa's eyes staring at him, only at his back now.

He never bargained for this nervousness.

What the hell was the matter with him?

CHAPTER SIX

Light rain was falling by the time Callum got to Marshal Rigby's large, white-painted clapboard dwelling on the eastern outskirts of town. All the way there he vowed the lapses in his demeanour, such as the one he experienced in Jedidiah's Chapel of Rest and when he came out of the door, could not be allowed to happen again. But the resolution did not seem to be working. His gut was still feeling as though it had a dozen knots tied in it and his imagination was still conjuring up the vision of Pa's steely eyes staring up at him.

As he approached the marshal's house, he saw the inside was lit with warm yellow lamplight, which was illuminating the rain-filled mist of the night outside. Through the clean net curtains he could see Ma, Betty Lou, Kate Rigby and Larson Rigby were gathered in the parlour.

As he got close to the gallery's shingle-roof shelter he could hear the rain pattering on it with steady noise. He mounted the two steps to the stoop and took advantage of its cover. While beating his damp hat against his right thigh he rapped on the jamb with the other hand and stood waiting for the fly door and outer door to open. When the outer door opened Larson Rigby peered out. Callum noticed the marshal's craggy face was hollower than usual and was clearly troubled. 'Callum,' Rigby said, with some relief, 'come in. Your mother is in the parlour with Betty Lou.' He shook his head. 'This is a terrible business, Callum, truly terrible.'

Callum said, the lie he was about to tell knotting up his guts afresh, 'I can't think of a worse one,' he said. 'Is Jim here?'

'No, he's out asking questions in town.' Rigby sighed, as if in exasperation. 'I tried to explain to him Mal and me had done all that, but you know what he's like, he has to find these things out for himself. Stubborn as a mule.'

'Yeah,' Callum said sourly, 'that's Jim all right.'

Rigby waved a hand. 'Well, you'd better come through, Callum.'

Ma and Betty Lou met him in the hall. They threw themselves into his open arms and he hugged them close. After moments he said, 'I don't know what to say, Ma. I just can't take it in.'

'You're here, that's enough,' Sarah McKendry said.

Then they stood there in the passageway hugging, the women weeping soft tears on to Callum's deep chest. Rigby took the opportunity to ease past them. He entered the parlour. There he asked his wife Kate if she'd make coffee. 'Of course,' she said and went into the kitchen. Meanwhile, Callum, Ma and Betty Lou stood there in the hall, still in that sorrow-filled embrace. When they finally broke up Rigby came to them and led the two ladies into the parlour and got them seated.

'Coffee will be ready in a minute,' he said.

Also seated, Callum stared up at the Flat Rock marshal and again tried to control his jangling nerves. This was the charade he would have to maintain. He never figured on this kind of reaction when he planned the murders. He always reckoned he was tougher than that. But it seemed a man never really knew himself until he was tested. He made a huge effort to get his nerves in line. He said, 'Who could have done such a thing, Larson?'

Rigby let out a frustrated sigh and shook his head. 'God knows. I wish I could say I was on to him, but I can't. It's a total dead end. Whoever did it knew exactly what he was about.'

'You think it's one man, then?'

'My instincts tell me so.' The marshal's stare was hard. 'Dammit, Callum, there's no rhyme or reason to it. As well you know, John was a liked and well-respected figure on this range.'

Callum said, 'Surely someone saw *something?*'

God Almighty, he never knew he could lie like this.

Rigby shook his head again. 'Nary a thing; we've asked every person likely to know: bar staff, night owls, calico queens going home to their shacks. Just nothing. They were all in a hurry, trying to get to

42

where they were going before the rain got started, probably already at home, most of them. The night life here ain't exactly Dodge City on a Saturday night.'

'I reckon,' Callum said. 'I gather from what you say Jim seems to think you ain't trying hard enough; not asked the right questions.'

Rigby shrugged. 'I can understand his attitude to a degree. He's shocked; he's upset; and we all know him. Once he gets his teeth into something he just won't let go. And this was his father that was murdered. Even so, I have tried to tell him he should let the law deal with lawman's business, that he should look to his family's needs and not go over ground Mal and me have already trod. Nevertheless, he just doesn't seem to cotton on to that, seems to have this quirk in him to go it alone.'

Larson stared with fierce grey eyes. 'Dammit, Callum, nobody in this basin wants that killer more than Mal and me but can I get Jim to appreciate that? No. He seems to think he is the only man in this basin able to track down that no good son of a bitch.'

Callum said, 'That's Jim.'

Kate Rigby came into the parlour carrying a tray with a tall coffee pot on it. She set it down on the large polished round table in the centre of the room. Then she returned to the kitchen and came back carrying a tray with cups and saucers on it. She placed it down on the table beside the tray with the coffee pot on it. She silently poured and distributed the stimulant. Then she said, looking around hopefully. 'There's cookies if anybody's feeling hungry.'

Sarah and Betty Lou's heads shook and went down. They looked into the contents of their cups, tragedy and shock still written all over their tear-stained features. Seeing their misery, Kate sat down on the settee between them and put her arms around their shuddering shoulders. 'Oh, God,' she said, 'Sarah, Betty Lou, I just don't know what to say or do to help.'

Sarah closed her right hand over Kate's and said quietly, 'You're here, that's enough.'

Callum fidgeted with his cup, and then lifted it off the saucer. He took it trembling to his lips. Jesus in heaven, what had he done? To Betty Lou, in particular. Would she understand when he explained his plans? Again he took a grip on himself. He said, 'How long has Jim been gone? Don't he know he's wanted here?'

The marshal of Flat Rock frowned as he observed Callum's shaking hands then he looked up at him. 'Are you feeling all right, son? You don't look good.'

Callum said, 'How can I be all right, Pa all cut up like that?'

A knock on the door interrupted Rigby's reply and he excused himself and went out. Callum heard the two doors open; again heard the rain pattering on the gallery roof and again cease when the two doors closed. Then there was the noise of a wet coat being shed and shaken. After moments a man six feet three inches tall, his shoulders near touching each side of the door, came into the parlour and took in the scene with blue, keen eyes. Callum Bowden stared at his substitute brother. He did not like him. He did not like his self-assured manner, his occasional arrogance, his relentless spirit, his formidable abilities with rope and gun. The sight of Jim McKendry once more stirred up the raw ambition in him to own the Rafter M. He swamped his fear. He said, 'Where's you been? Ma and Betty Lou want you here, dammit.'

Jim McKendry drifted his gaze onto Callum and said, 'Well, howdy to you, too, brother.'

Sarah McKendry, her head suddenly coming up, said, 'Boys, for God's sake, put your differences aside for now.'

Marshal Rigby, who was now leaning on the mantelshelf said, if a little sarcastically, 'How did it go, Jim? Find anything? Not that Mal and me have most likely found it anyway.'

Jim turned his gaze on to the marshal. 'I'd apologize if it was in me to go about stepping on your toes, Larson, but the fact of the matter is, I have found something. Pop Eye Cameron, him who keeps bar over at the Cumberland Saloon, says he was having his usual nightcap when he looked out the saloon window around two in the morning and saw a man dressed all in black come down the back stairs of the High Life Hotel and—'

Rigby interrupted, tartly, 'Is that so? Well, for your information, Jim, Mal and me have already talked with Pop Eye and we have decided what he saw was of no significance.' Larson paused and sighed heavily. 'Look, Jim, I appreciate your efforts but will you now let the law of this town deal with the policing of it?'

Jim said, 'He's my pa, Larson. And you'd better understand right now I will not rest until that murderous dog is hanging by his neck in the centre of town. I'll even build the gallows myself, if need be.'

Rigby said, with clear emotion, 'D'you think I don't want that, too, son? Why, your pa and me were friends for high on forty years; we rode together as Texas Rangers for ten years. We fought side by side as Texas Riflemen right up until that Appomattox humiliation.'

The marshal paused, sighed and waited, as if to calm himself and settle his obviously deep rooted feelings. Then he waved a hand. 'Jim, right now, this isn't the time or the place to be doing this. You now have responsibilities and your mother and your sister need you. Go back to the ranch. Let me and Mal deal with this.'

As if to pour oil on troubled waters Kate Rigby came forward smiling and carrying a cup of coffee. She handed it to Jim. 'Here, this will warm you up,' she said. Then she added, 'Now, where are you planning on staying the night, Jim? Sarah and Betty Lou will be staying here with us, of course.' She made a gesture of apology. 'I'd like to offer you and Callum a bed, but we don't have enough. However, you and Callum are more than welcome to use the two settees.'

Jim felt the soft spot he had for his mother's long-time friend warm him. He said, 'Thanks, Kate, but I've already got a room at the High Life Hotel. I shall be riding out early in the morning and I don't want to disturb anybody. I intend making some enquiries on the range.'

Callum said, 'What about Ma, Betty Lou, the ranch? Just like you, to run out on your responsibilities.'

Jim bunched his fists, turned, his stare steel bright. 'Damn you, Callum! Shut that big mouth of yours.'

Ma's sharp reprimand cut the air across the parlour, 'Boys, that's enough! Show some respect.'

Jim continued to stare at Callum for some moments before he turned to his mother and sister. They were still huddled together on the settee. Betty Lou was sobbing, Ma staring up at him, hard.

Guilt bit at him for a moment then he said, 'You're right, Ma, but it still don't change a thing.' He went over and kissed her tenderly in the cheek, then Betty Lou. Then he added, quietly, 'Ma, that killer is still out there, and until he is caught I will know no peace. I reckon Pa will understand.'

He turned and stared at Callum. 'So long, brother.'

Callum grunted and looked sulkily into the glowing fire. Jim now turned to Larson Rigby, standing by the fireplace, and said quietly, 'Thank you for all you are doing, Larson.'

Rigby came away from the fireplace and took him by the arm and said quietly, 'I'll see you out, son.'

When they got to the door he went on, 'If you do happen on to something, come to me and we'll get a posse out. Don't try anything on your own. That man's a killer.'

Jim said, 'Can't promise a thing, Larson, I'll play as I see it.'

Rigby snorted, glared at him angrily, but kept his voice low, 'Just as stubborn as your father, Goddamnit!'

Jim attempted a half-smile, though he knew there was nothing to smile about at this tragic time. 'I'll take that as a compliment.'

Outside the house he found the rain had stopped. Even so, he hunched deeper into his range coat. Underfoot was a mess of sticky mud and the sky above was pitch black and threatening more rain. On top of that a raw, stiff breeze was blowing in from Wolf's Head Basin. He pulled down his worn, sweat-stained Stetson and leaned into the wind's keen edge. He headed for the High Life Hotel and hopefully Lisette Simon's warm, tender arms – the woman that had been part of his life for nigh on two years now; the woman he loved with a deep passion.

But she did not fill the whole of his thoughts. There were other thoughts, too. Like having Pa's killer on the gallows before the week was out.

CHAPTER SEVEN

It was three months on now. It was ten o'clock in the morning. Jim was in Larson Rigby's sparsely furnished office. He was staring across the spur-scarred oak desk, which was littered with papers. The rays of the hot August sun were slanting in through the dust-rimed windows. Flat Rock's ageing lawman was playing with the pen in his hands and was staring back at him. He was saying:

'Dammit, for the last time, Jim, let it go. There just isn't going to be a resolution to it. As I have already said a hundred times: John's death was bad, awful, terrible and I wish to God I could find a solution to it, but we've got nothing to go on, nary a thing.' He threw down his pen in disgust and leaned back. 'I don't like it any more than you do, but there it is.' The marshal's frustration was clear to see as he turned and stared moodily out of the window at the busy Main Street.

Larson Rigby, Jim conceded, had worked tirelessly these past three months to ensure justice got done for his father. So had he. And, as Rigby had said, there was nothing to show for their efforts; just dead ends to every enquiry made. And the biggest devil in it was, now the big shock was over and John McKendry was three months in his grave, things were settling back to normal here in Wolf's Head Basin. Like it or not, the consensus of opinion was the dead were dead and life went on, sad as that might be for some. Even Ma and Betty Lou appeared to be coming to terms with that harsh reality. But not Jim McKendry. His disappointment at not finding the killer was still grinding away at his vitals, as if it was corn under a millstone. He could not let the matter go. He did not want to let it go. And there was another development recently he didn't like, out there at the Rafter M.

Callum and Betty Lou were now real close. Jim knew there had always been certain feelings going on between them, more or less since Callum became part of the family all those years ago. Kids' stuff at first, which he often teased Callum about, but these days it appeared to be serious and adult. Jim admitted he did not like it. Perhaps it was because he did not like Callum Bowden; or maybe it was because he had become overpossessive, or overprotective towards his sister now Pa was dead. However, if he was to be totally honest with himself, he did not want Betty Lou to make what he thought was a bad decision, because marriage to Callum Bowden certainly seemed to be on the cards, if he was reading the trends correctly.

Not only that, while he had been riding all over Montana Territory and beyond, chasing down half rumours, searching low-life dives in sleazy and dangerous outlaw towns trying to run down Pa's killer, Callum had been at the Rafter M greasing up to Ma and Betty Lou, or so it appeared the few times he had visited the ranch these past months. However, when he complained to Callum about his lack of interest in finding Pa's murderer, he usually got angry, said he was just as interested as his goddamn substitute brother was, but somebody had to be around the place to look after things; somebody needed to be there to pick up the pieces, offer what solace and comfort the grieving women at the Rafter M still needed to prevent them from breaking down completely. Jim stared moodily at the bare board wall of the marshal's office opposite him.

He felt deep frustration course through him. Even Ma was coming round to saying he had become obsessed with finding Pa's killer and that he was insulting the marshal by keep poking his nose in – *the family's long-time friend, Jim,* she had reminded him. However, it was over supper three weeks ago at the Rafter M that things finally came to a head. Callum had stared at him across the table and said, 'Dammit, Jim, Ma's right; Marshal Rigby and Deputy Delaney should be left to deal with the situation in their own way. That is what we pay taxes for. What's more, I'm getting sick and tired of having to run the Rafter M on my own.'

Jim glared back at him and barked, 'Then let Bat

Losey look after things, if you ain't up to it.'

Bat Losey was the Rafter M straw boss. He came up from Texas with Pa in '66. Pa always said he would trust Losey with the ranch and his life, and had done on more than one occasion. In particular, when the Hunkpapa Sioux made a dawn raid on the ranch spring of '74. Pa was out bringing in the cows for Ma to milk later, confident Bat had his eyes peeled. There had been Indian trouble for some time.

Bat was standing hidden in the shadows of the bunkhouse. The lamps were out. Bat was staring out over the vast rolling acres of the Rafter M, which were lying chill and dew-laden and mystical in the light of the early morning dawn.

First thing Pa knew was Bat Losey shooting the Hunkpapa brave that was attempting to sneak up on him along the corral rails, knife in hand, ready to kill him and peel his scalp.

The noise of Bat Losey's Remington cap-and-ball immediately roused the men in the bunkhouse and all hell broke lose. In the end, Pa, Bat and the boys managed to kill three more Hunkpapas before the raiding party of ten, reduced to six by the time the skirmish was over, lit out shrieking and whooping and empty handed.

Jim continued to stare at his surrogate brother; happy his bitter reply had shut Callum up.

The rest of the meal was eaten in silence. The only thing marring it were Ma's few reproving looks aimed at the both of them. It was when Jim was preparing to return to Flat Rock that Ma took him to one side and said, 'Jim, this thing between you and Callum has gone far enough. Put your differences aside. We need you here at the Rafter M, pulling your weight. And I think it is about time you accepted the fact that your father's killer is not going to be found and settle for that.'

Jim stared into his mother's earnest, pleading eyes. It hurt him to see her so anxious. But he said, 'Ma, until that murderer is hanging from the gallows I'm going to build for him, or dropping dead before my smoking gun, I'm going to carry on. The good name of the McKendrys demands it; Pa would demand it if he was still here.'

Ma was silent for long moments before she said, 'That was way below the belt, Jim, suggesting I don't. I'm just being realistic.'

Jim felt immediate regret, nevertheless he said, 'I'm sorry, Ma, but that's the way it is with me.'

Jim seldom said sorry, but Ma was different. He revered her. She gave him life, she gave him meaning, and she gave him soul. It near tore his guts out to see her shake her head and turn back to the house, clearly in despair.

Moodily, Jim stared out of the law office window. Was he so obsessed? Was he developing into this cold, intractable man that could see nothing beyond vengeance? But dammit, nobody seemed to understand the failure to catch Pa's killer was eating at him like a cancer, that it was a wrong done to the whole of the McKendry clan and he would not be able to rest until the matter was resolved, even if it took a lifetime? Eventually, he turned his gaze on to Marshal Rigby. 'Some day he'll surface, Larson, and when that day comes I'll get him.'

Marshal Rigby sighed, met his gaze and said, 'Jim, get back to the ranch. Your ma and Betty Lou desperately need you there and it isn't fair on Callum, keep burdening him with all that responsibility. It's your ranch now. You own the place; it's your responsibility, so go see to its needs. If anything turns up you'll be the first to know, I promise you.'

Jim got up out of the chair, his lips a tight thin line. It was like swallowing bitter gall to have to admit closure to this. A feeling of utter defeat descended over him like a death shroud. Nevertheless he sighed and said, 'Maybe you're right. Larson.'

Rigby nodded, his grim, craggy face grave. 'You know I am. Now go home, Jim, and join the human race again.'

Jim stared at the lawman for some moments, stung by the last remark, but decided not to answer it. Larson always meant well and he could appreciate Rigby's frustration must be similar to his own.

He touched the brim of his hat. He said, 'My regards to Kate, Larson.'

Rigby's hard face softened. 'Thanks, son; I'll pass them on.'

CHAPTER EIGHT

Jim went out into the bright morning sunlight, which was smashing down heat on to the ankle-deep stretch of dust that was, in this dry month of August, Main Street. He headed for the Saddleman's Rest with one thing in mind. He needed a beer, maybe two, even three. No, dammit, he needed a barrel full of the stuff to get rid of this taste of defeat in his mouth. He just was not ready yet to go back to Ma's hurt looks and Betty Lou's growing disdain. But the real truth was, he couldn't go on letting Callum handle things at the Rafter M – going over Bat Losey's head on vital things, even though he appeared to be doing so with Ma's full approval, which Losey, though no doubt reluctantly, was accepting out of respect for Ma.

The stage from Elk Butte, the big mining town a hundred miles north and close to the Canadian border, came to a halt in a cloud of dust in front of the Wells Fargo office. The horses, Jim saw, were dusty and streaked with foam and sweat. They stamped and snorted as they came to a stop, still excited after their long run from the last way station fifteen miles north on Beaver Lodge Creek.

Driver Slim Brewster and shotgun guard Ollie Munstein came down from the driver's seat, grunting and cursing the heat. On terra firma, Slim swung open the coach door and bawled, 'Flat Rock, folks, half an hour's stop. For those travelling on, vittles are laid on in the High Life restaurant. There are also facilities to tidy up. You may also use the Crapper if you so wish, courtesy of the High Life.'

Smiling at Slim's forthright information, Jim turned from gazing at Brewster to see the change horses were being urged up the street from the Wells Fargo barns and corrals, situated on the northeast outskirts of town. The stirring event of the stage's arrival now over, Jim prepared to resume his walk to the Saddle Man's Rest.

What brought him to an abrupt halt was the sight of elegantly dressed Lisette Simon, his heart's desire, demurely stepping down from the stage, following the other five travel-stained passengers. Now she stood there patting her emerald-green gown free of most of the dust it had gathered on the journey to Flat Rock. Lisette Simon owned the High Life Hotel. She won it off Big Bill Sykes in an all-night poker game three years ago. Since then she had made a real good job of running the place, had won a lot of admiration in town doing it, though not from all quarters.

There were rumours she had once been the star singer in one of Denver's plushest theatres. There was also range gossip she'd dealt cards in some of the hottest poker games going during Dodge City's rip-roaring go-to-hell days. Indeed, she had made a sizeable fortune in the process but lost it one night on the turn of a card. Now Lisette was a very shrewd business lady, older and wiser, and not likely to gamble everything on the turn of a card ever again. On top of that she played the stock market with some skill and turned the rundown High Life Hotel of Big Bill Sykes's days into a thriving, profit-making concern. Also, she lit up this sleepy town of Flat Rock with her bold, feisty, but always elegant ways. The only element in town to disapprove was Flat Rock's Ladies League for Christian Purity. But then, thinking on it, those august ladies complained about damn near everything, Jim decided.

Relishing the sight of her, he looked her up and down. It was well known hereabouts they had a relationship. God knew why, for Lisette could have the pick of Wolf's Head Basin and way beyond, if she wanted it. Jim knew very well all she needed to do was snap her fingers and they'd all come running.

When she saw him her smile, made with full, inviting lips, lit up her aristocratic, some would say, slightly haughty features. Her plucked eyebrows, darkly pencilled below her peacock-plumed, wide-brimmed black hat, arched over her robin egg blue eyes, as if in enquiry. Her auburn curls hung down in ringlets from under her hat. She looked cool, even in this intense heat.

'Well, well,' she said, as she came close, 'The

mighty Jim McKendry. Still chasing after killers, lover?'

'It isn't a joke, Lisette.'

'It wasn't meant to be.'

To change the subject he said, 'I didn't know you were out of town.'

'That is understandable,' she said, 'seeing as you're never in town two days together.' She cocked a pencilled eyebrow. 'God, but you look terrible. Fancy a drink?'

Well, he was heading for refreshment, and Lisette Simon's suite of rooms at the High Life definitely had much more appeal than the stuffy, tobacco-smoke-filled and cow-dung-reeking atmosphere of the Saddleman's Rest. What was more, he had not seen Lisette Simon more than four times in the past three months. The sight of her now in all her curvaceous glory sent his blood roaring through his veins like a torrent. So he could not believe what was coming out of his mouth when he said, 'Mind if I pass? Just ain't in the mood right now.'

If she was insulted she did not show it. She stared at him with those clear, thoughtful blue eyes and then she touched his arm and said, 'Stop beating yourself up, Jim; bend a little. You're driving yourself crazy with this thing.'

He caught the tantalizing hint of her expensive perfume. The lovely Lisette Simon; originally of French-Canadian descent, her ancestry in that North Country going back over three hundred years. God, he really loved this woman. His resolve, as he knew it would do even if she pushed her invitation only a smidgeon, melted under her ravishing charm.

'Dammit, you're right,' he said. 'It was crazy of me to think otherwise.'

She smiled and nudged him in the ribs. 'Now you're talking.'

At that moment Slim Brewster came up carrying her two carpetbags. 'There ye go, Miss Simon, safe and sound. Want for me to carry them in?'

She smiled at the grizzled driver and then mischievously cocked an eye toward Jim and said, 'I would normally, Slim, but this time I reckon I've already got me a porter. But thanks for the offer anyway. I'll see to it there's a drink on the bar next time you call in the High Life.'

Slim Brewster beamed. 'By dally, I'll hold you to that, missy,' he said, 'soon as I get back from Butte.'

Jim took the bags off Brewster and escorted her across the street. They entered the High Life. As they crossed the lounge she said to the deskman, 'Get somebody to bring a bottle to my room, Charlie. You know the brand. And get Fanny to hot up some bath water and bring it up.'

Bald-headed, perspiring and celluloid-collared Charlie smiled and said, 'Yes, ma'am. Right away.'

He cocked a meaningful eye towards Jim and slyly grinned. Jim returned it with a dagger-like look, which Charlie ignored.

Lisette Simon's suite of rooms was on the first floor, overlooking Main Street. They were familiar to Jim. He had spent a lot of time in them over the past two years. He would have made an honest woman of her a long time ago and had made moves to do so by proposing on several occasions, even though Ma did not approve of the union. But Pa sure did and that was good enough for Jim McKendry. But, dammit, every time he asked her she would smile in that coy, but enticing, way she had and say, 'Not right now, lover; but maybe one day, huh?'

Pa said he could not understand the woman. Ma kept her peace but looked relieved. However, it hurt Jim to have his ego bruised so often. Nevertheless, it did not deter him from continuing to make constant overtures in the hope she would capitulate. Most every Friday evening he took flowers up to her rooms. Sometimes, on special occasions, he took chocolates. Occasionally, when strolling players were in town, he took her to the town's dancehall where the actors more often than not staged their plays, that being the most suitable venue. They also attended hoedowns in the barns of local ranchers as well as real dances with polkas and waltzes at Fort Wilson, five miles west of town. And afterwards the icing on the cake was an invitation to stay the night. Not only that, Lisette would serve a slap-up supper, with real French champagne, properly chilled. God, man, what a woman!

In her rooms he put down the carpetbags and settled down into one of the comfortable satin-padded, pale blue chairs. He pulled out a stogie from the silver case he kept them in and lit it with a sulphur match, ignited by his thumbnail. He pulled at it until it glowed red at the tip. Relaxing fully now, he watched the blue smoke rise to the ceiling as he wafted out the match. He returned the case to the inside pocket of his range coat. Meanwhile, Lisette went into her sweet-smelling boudoir where they had weekly made love joyfully and whole-heartedly until Pa got killed.

He heard satins rustle and water splash. She came back five minutes later wrapped in a sleek-fitting green dressing gown that showed off her feminine contours to the full. She looked refreshed. She must have used the water from the washstand jug and bowl and splashed it over her face and upper body before she repaired her make-up. He lit another stogie and passed it over. She took it with a smile and curled up on the chaise-longue across from him. Elegantly, she drew in smoke and inhaled. Exhaling, her blue eyes appraised him through the smoke. Her question, when it came, surprised him because the subject had kept them apart for so long. He thought it would have been the last thing she'd have wanted to bring up right now.

She said, 'Have you got anything on your pa's killer yet?'

He looked at her intently. 'No. Why?'

The rap on the door interrupted. Lisette said, 'Come in.'

A barman Jim knew entered carrying a tray with a bottle and two glasses on it. She pointed to a small table.

'Put it down there, Edmund.'

'Yes, ma'am.' Edmund did as he was asked and let himself out.

Lisette rose from the chaise-longue, picked up the bottle, which, Jim saw, according to the brand on the label, was one of the finest Kentucky bourbons. She poured large measures into the two cut-glass tumblers. She passed one to him and then reclined again and sipped from her glass, her stogie held high in the air between the first two fingers of her elegant left hand.

Meanwhile, Jim sipped of the bourbon and smacked his lips. 'That sure hits the spot,' he said. Then he looked around. 'Just like old times, uh?'

Her eyebrows arched. 'You're planning to stay a while?'

He grinned. 'That an invitation?'

Her tantalizing stare held his. 'You know it is. Dammit, Jim, I've missed you. It's near six weeks since we . . . you know.'

He broadened his grin. 'Been counting, uh?'

She put down her half-full glass on the tray and placed the stogie on the lip of the tray beside it. Then she stared at him intently, almost as if she was searching into his very soul. Then she said, 'I don't know whether I ought to tell you this, lover.'

He stared at her. His instinct was telling him whatever it was could be important. He said, 'Dammit, Lisette, if this is something to do with Pa's killer I'd like you to come straight out with it.'

She stared back at him and said, 'Why should I if you're going to go running all over God's creation

62

again chasing shadows, maybe getting yourself killed?' Her blue eyes now pleaded with him. 'Leave it to the law, Jim, that is what they're there for.'

But the fever was in him again. He grabbed her arm. 'Dammit, Lisette, if you know something out with it.'

She pulled away from him, her eyes big and round. 'Why?' Her voice turned harsh. Her stare now reflected the hurt in her. 'You're obsessed, Jim, don't you know that?' Impulsively then, her hand caressed his face. Her gaze grew intense because of the fear for his safety that dwelled in her. 'Oh, darling, drop this. Go back to the ranch. Get back to being my Jim again. If you react to this like I think you will it's going to be another dumb journey with nothing at the end only more frustration.'

'What is it, Lisette?' His voice rasped with the demand in it.

She averted her gaze and stared for some moments at the flower-patterned wallpaper covering the street wall. Then she turned and looked at him boldly. 'OK,' she said. 'As you must have guessed, I've just got back from Elk Butte. There has been a murder up there, similar to your father's. Some fellow got his throat cut from ear to ear. The report in the *Elk Butte Courier* says it was a carbon copy of the one that laid your father low.' She paused, bent and fumbled about in one of her carpetbags he'd placed beside the chaise-longue. She lifted out the four-page newssheet and thrust it at him.

'Here, read it for yourself and go to hell!'

Despite her bitter remark he studied it, avidly, devouring every word. It was the best lead to hit Flat Rock in three months. He found he was trembling with excitement as he got to his feet. He looked down at her and said, 'It's got to be him, Lisette, got to be.'

She said, scorn in her tone, 'It has? How perceptive.'

He said, looking at her pleadingly. 'You know I've got to go, honey.'

Her full lips curled up in scorn. 'Have you?' She turned away from him and stared at the wallpaper once more. 'Then don't let me keep you.'

He could tell she was deeply hurt and a torrent of guilt poured through him. Even so he said, 'I've got to follow it up, sweetheart; I know no other way.'

She said, 'The hell you have.' She pressed her clasped hands in her lap, turned her head as if she could not get far enough away from him and could not bear looking at him. After moments she said, her voice taut with emotion, 'Just go, Jim, before I scream the place down.'

He hesitated. He stared at the back of her head, at the auburn ringlets hanging limp with sweat on to her graceful neck. He didn't want to lose her, did not want to hurt her, not in a million years.

He felt this sudden tremendous urge to take her in his arms and to kiss her and say he would stay and to hell with it, but instead he said, 'I'm real sorry, honey, it's just the way I am.'

'Go to hell, I said!' But it was a deeply hurt remark,

64

not at all a curse.

Feeling like a whipped cur, he went across the room to the door. He opened it and stepped through the threshold, closing it quietly behind him. He walked along the carpeted landing and down the stairs. He crossed the lounge; Charlie's eyes followed him all the way, as if he could not believe he was walking out on so beautiful a woman, and so soon. But he was and he went out into the hot sunlight.

CHAPTER NINE

Jim found a brooding gloom was descending over him as he paced along the street. He would have liked to leave Lisette Simon thinking kindly of him, but why should she? He was obsessed and she knew he was.

Staring grimly ahead, he headed for Henry Baron's Stalling, Hay and Grain – Manure Delivered. He paid Henry stalling fees owed and then saddled up his dun horse. On his way out of town he stopped off at Freddie Jackson's Mercantile and got enough victuals for the three-day ride. Half an hour later he was heading out, using the Wells Fargo stage trail for Elk Butte.

Late afternoon three days on and well into the hills, he rode down the mining town's bustling First Street. The Rockies were bulked big, black and white-tipped far to the west.

Huge ore wagons rolled past him to the stamping mills, which were a constant crashing noise in the distance. In town, honky-tonk pianos jingled and miners caroused in the wide-open saloons, or fought with fisticuffs on the streets, or lay in drunken stupors on the sidewalk.

The marshal's office, he found, was open and he walked into the stuffy atmosphere. He introduced himself and then held the *Elk Butte Courier* almost under the lawman's nose.

Sitting behind the desk in his swivel chair, Marshal Ernest Rimmer looked up at him with keen grey eyes and then leaned forward and took the newssheet. He glanced at it briefly and then put it on the desk in front of him. He waved Jim into the swivel chair the other side of the desk.

'You're Jim McKendry, right?'

'Yeah.'

'What's on your mind?'

'The front page; read it.'

'I have, six days ago.'

'And?'

Rimmer stared. 'And, what?'

Jim waved an impatient hand. 'How's it going . . . the investigation? Have you got anybody for the killing?'

Rimmer sighed heavily. He sat back in his battered chair and twirled his pen between his long, bony fingers. Then he said, 'I've been expecting you, McKendry. Larson Rigby wired me day before yesterday saying you'd be calling. Well, we've done all the investigating we can on this business. We've come up with nothing. I've already wired what details we have down to Larson . . . seeing as he's the law down there and has been chasing down a similar killing in Flat Rock.' Rimmer leaned forward now. 'McKendry, what I advise you to do is to go back home and ask Larson about it. I'm a busy man.'

Stung by that abrupt dismissal, Jim got to his feet. 'Dammit, Rimmer, the bastard that done this killing is the man who killed my father.'

The marshal hard stare searched his. 'You're jumping to conclusions. How d'you know it's the same man?'

'I'd put money on it,' Jim said. 'Hotel room, the middle of the night, his throat slit from ear to ear, what more do you want?'

'It could've been a copy-cat killing,' Rimmer said. 'The *Elk Butte Courier* covered your pa's killing in detail at the time. The killer could have picked up on that and used it to put us off the scent.' Rimmer fiddled with his pen some more and sighed. 'Look, McKendry, I'm sorry about your father. I knew him well. John was a fine, decent man, salt of the earth. And because of that our investigations into this death have been thorough, in case we found a connection we could use. But the truth of it is, we haven't. We've hit a brick wall, just like Larson Rigby did – and you, from what I hear. McKendry, whoever did this killing knew exactly what he was doing. Nobody saw or heard a damned thing.'

'Somebody must have seen something,' Jim said.

Rimmer glared and said, bitterly, 'Did anybody see anything at Flat Rock?'

Jim opened his mouth to reply, but Rimmer held

up his hand to silence him and said, 'I'll answer that for you. No. Am I right?' Rimmer tightened his lips into a grim line and put down his pen. 'Look, McKendry, I've had two deputies working on this case for three days. In the end I had to say enough. The reason? We have killings happen every other day in this town. What's one more, for Christ's sake?'

Faced with that, Jim searched desperately for other avenues to explore. When one occurred he said, 'What's his family doing about it?'

Rimmer offered what could be construed as a cynical smile. 'Still living the good life in Philadelphia, is my guess. Over the wires, all that was requested was to have his body sent home. From that I figure, the will is in their favour. And because of *that*, I figure they do not want to know anything else.'

'Was he robbed?'

'No. There was a thousand dollars in bills on him.'

'Pa wasn't robbed, either,' Jim said. 'D'you think it was a contract killing?'

'Maybe,' Rimmer said. He leaned forward, picked up his pen and examined it as if it was some oracle that might provide him with some answers. Then he said, 'Look, it's like this; the fellow that got killed wasn't liked around here, hated by some. And it was common knowledge he killed a man – though nothing could be proved – and jumped his claim, the claim that has made him a rich man, or did.' Rimmer shrugged, studied the pen some more. 'I have been working on the theory that maybe the man he killed had relatives and they've finally tracked him down and taken their revenge.' Rimmer's look now held conviction as Jim met it. 'But whichever way it was, that bastard got what he deserved and I'll shed no tears. Even so, a killing is a killing and it was done in my area of jurisdiction. And that being the case, if you are staying on and you do come up with anything, let me know and I'll afford you any assistance I can. In the meantime, you're on your own.'

There was finality in Rimmer's tone and Jim saw no way around it. However, he recognized he was tacitly being given a free hand – within the law, of course. He said,

'Fair enough, Rimmer.'

Rimmer's stare was neutral. 'Glad you see it that way.'

Out on the street Jim threaded his way through the crowds of carousing miners. He was hardly aware of them. He needed to organize. First off, he must look for a place to rest his head when he was through asking his questions. But at every hotel, shack, fleapit, doghouse, and plain stinking dump the answer was the same: they were full to the rafters. Only one scruffy, bristled, rib-scratching ugly bastard offered him a place, provided he did not mind sleeping four in a bed.

Jim declined the invitation. An infestation of fleas and bed bugs was not what he was looking for right now, or ever. And checking on the exorbitant prices of what half-decent food he came across, he finally settled for a supper of beans and bacon cooked on a campfire beside the gently flowing Assiniboine Creek – the tree-lined stream he crossed on the ride into Elk Butte, fifteen minutes' ride out of town. As yet it looked as though the placer or hard rock miners swarming over these hills had not exploited it yet, which surprised him.

Meanwhile, after a full hour of dead-end enquiry into the mine owner's brutal death, using names of possible witnesses supplied by the editor of the *Elk Butte Courier* and Rimmer's three deputies, he came up with nothing. In the face of that bitter result he decided he needed a large drink, the glass filled up several times.

He found the Miner's Refuge north of town was quiet at this hour – barely a dozen men in the long room. He entered and immediately recoiled. After breathing in the clean air of the hills and prairie for the past three days, the stale atmosphere within hit him like a slap in the face. There was an aroma of cheap alcohol, tobacco and the rank stink of sweat from unwashed men.

Reaching about the middle of the long mahogany bar, he discovered at the back of it was the painting of a fulsome and reclining nude, which was hanging prominently on the wall amid a staggering array of glasses and bottles.

He bought and took an exorbitantly priced bottle of branded whiskey to a corner table, along with a shot glass. He sat down, took a cigar out of his silver case and put it in his mouth and then returned the case to his inside coat pocket. He poured a liberal

71

measure of the yellow-brown liquid, lighted his cigar and then sipped gratefully on the smooth liquor while he listened to an arguing bunch miners playing poker at a nearby table.

After a couple of minutes, while he let the whiskey warm and calm him, Jim looked despairingly out at the street through the open half-glass doors. For all his careful questioning just now, he had come up with nothing. He was fast losing all hope of ever catching the murderous bastard that killed his father. Lisette Simon was right. He should have kept his nose out, let the law deal with it.

He was about to pour another whiskey when he became aware of the man standing by his table, drink in hand, looking down at him with glittering, dark eyes. He appeared to be in his mid forties, consumptive, and unarmed. Jim also observed he was dressed mostly in black: black suit, white shirt, with a black cravat. On his narrow head was a black, wide brimmed, flat-crowned hat.

Jim decided he could be some preacher, or funeral director, or even a theatrical dude trying to sell tickets for the latest drama to hit town; a cliche for every no-good baddy portrayed in the modern theatre. Mining towns like Elk Butte attracted all kinds of oddball humanity, as well as groups of travelling actors, in town to act out the latest melodramas to hit the West. There were always genuine attempts, when the town's coffers began to fill and men grew rich, to try and bring some semblance of culture to these lawless boom towns.

Indeed, there were two theatres in town that he knew of. There could be more.

Jim stared up at the man standing by his table. He said, 'I don't want no tickets, mister, if that's what you're peddling.'

The man frowned his puzzlement. 'Tickets?' he said. Then, after moments, his face made a good imitation of lighting up. 'Oh, yes.' He smiled, exposing a row of white, tombstone-shaped teeth. 'I see what you mean. Well, no, sir, I'm not selling tickets. Indeed, no. Allow me to introduce myself.' He offered a gloved hand. Jim took it reluctantly. 'My name is Christian van Otis and I believe you are looking for the man who killed your father?'

Jim straightened up in his chair, suspicion, as well as keen interest filling him. 'You believe right. Do you know something?'

'I could do, sir.'

'*Could do?*' A hint of anger rippled through Jim. 'Listen, friend, I'm not in the mood for games. If you've got some information give it or quit wasting my time. OK?'

Van Otis smiled once more, but his dark eyes were expressionless. As Jim gazed into those black orbs, they appeared to him to be without soul. Indeed, they had the look of a rattler studying its prey before striking; beady, pitiless. Every fibre in his body went on alert. But van Otis was saying, his voice surprisingly cultured and gentle, 'No, sir, I am not a time waster. In truth, I am far from that.' He raised thick, dark brows. 'The plain fact of the matter is, Mr

McKendry, I have been following your search to find your father's killer for some time – and with great interest, may I add. Now I feel it is time for me to consult with you.'

Jim said, 'Consult? You're still not making a deal of sense, mister. Start explaining.'

Van Otis smiled. 'I'll be only too happy to do so. I don't know whether you know this, but from the little I have been able to learn about the killer . . . he is of medium build, has blond hair and piercing blue eyes. He wears a six-gun but his forte – as we both very well know – is the knife.'

Forte? Jim frowned. What the hell was that? More suspicion filled him. He said, 'You seem to know a lot, friend; more than the law or me. Now, just what is your interest in this?'

'Very intense, I assure you,' van Otis said. 'The man you are seeking also killed my mother. I, too, need redress.'

The news sobered Jim. 'Well, that's a hell of a thing to bear, mister, I got to say.'

Van Otis sighed. 'Indeed, it is.'

Jim now searched for words. 'So, seeing as you know so much, d'you know where he is now? Have you got a name?'

'Alas, no, to both questions,' van Otis said. He sighed again. 'Believe me, I have worked tirelessly these past years, but have uncovered little about the man. Nevertheless, I have a suspicion he may be headed south for Flat Rock, after this latest killing here in Elk Butte. Let me explain. I am considered by some to be a psychic—'

Jim interrupted, 'A psychic, what the hell is that?'

Van Otis's look became grave. 'Why, a man who has the ability to anticipate things, forecast things if you like; see into the future, although scientists will assure you the whole thing is bunkum.'

Jim attempted a half-smile. Not only the scientists. However, he made an attempt to humour the man. 'Leastways you're honest, mister. Now what's this fellow going to do in Flat Rock?'

Van Otis shrugged his narrow shoulders. 'Another killing, I suppose. The vibrations are all there.'

Vibrations? That did it for Jim. The man was crazy. He did not know why he was wasting time with him. He got up, corked the bottle and put it in the patch pocket of his range coat. He said, 'Mister, I ain't got time for this.'

He began to stride toward the door, but van Otis raised a hand, alarm now in his black gaze. He said, 'Please, Mr McKendry, wait; I urge you to heed me, for it could be his target is another member of your family . . . perhaps even you. I implore you to listen to what I have to say. My abilities do have merit.'

Jim stopped mid-stride, his anger peaking. Over the months he'd had his fill of freaky people like van Otis coming up with half-ass talk, half-ass theories. He turned and grabbed the fellow by his coat lapels and drew him close. He looked into his black, expressionless eyes. He was a little surprised that they stared back, completely unafraid, for he knew he could be very intimidating when he was in this mood.

But van Otis did not seem to be in the least bit ruffled. Jim concluded, maybe he really *was* a half-wit? He let go of his suit and said, 'Mister, if you know something you'd better spit it out; I don't find this funny.'

Van Otis looked more than a little annoyed to have his well-cut suit so badly abused. He said, indignantly brushing down its front with bony hands, 'Funny is not what it is meant to be, Mr McKendry. I *do* have visions; I *do* anticipate things. Why, I do not know; it is one of the mysteries of life. But Mother always said it was because I *was* a psychic and I must accept whatever God has given me.'

Van Otis continued to dust down his suit, then he said, 'While the phenomenon is not recognized by a lot of learned people, others – those who dabble in the occult and even the common people – claim that it has a great deal of merit. And, much as I dislike admitting it, being a man of learning myself, I do possess this ability to see into the future and I do try to warn people of what is coming, when I can. But, if you choose not to accept my premonition, then there is little I can do about it. Nevertheless, it does fill me with some distress when you do not listen to my pleas.'

McKendry stared long and hard into those dark eyes before he said, 'Mister, you're something else; d'you know that?' He shoved van Otis aside. 'Now go and pedal your crazy trash somewhere else.'

Van Otis looked appalled and held out his arms. 'But, sir, I beseech you to listen to me. What I say

76

could save your life.'

Jim felt hot rage flush through him. He said, 'Mister, go to hell!'

Without waiting for an answer he strode across the sawdust-covered board floor and stepped out into the gathering dark. Soon he was heading for Assiniboine Creek. As planned, there he would make camp, have supper and no doubt sleep well, but always with one ear open, as was his habit when out on open range. Come sun-up he would head out for Flat Rock and to hell with that crazy bastard van Otis and his supposed psychic abilities. It was all bullshit. A man dealt with what was in front of him, not what was supposed to be in some crackpot's head.

Goddamnit!

CHAPTER TEN

Van Otis sat down in the chair Jim vacated. He smiled as he watched, with a cold, calculating black stare, McKendry stride out of the saloon door. To him this was just a cynical game. Harvard educated, until his expulsion, he liked to tease and, though absurd to most, because of his cultured background, yes, he did like to believe he had psychic abilities. But really, if he was to be brutally honest with himself, it was just this sardonic desire to sow the seeds of doubt in a potential victim that drove him on; get the man thinking about the possibility he was not immortal and that he might be facing death in the very near future. Which, logically, is what McKendry would be doing if Callum Bowden and his friend – the 'we' Bowden let slip at Santee Creek – needed another elimination carried out.

Van Otis continued to smile. Indeed, right now, cold deduction was telling him Jim McKendry must be Callum Bowden's next victim. Bowden was ambitious, wanted to become the owner of the Rafter

M; that would be plain to any thinking man. So Jim McKendry's elimination must be the next requirement. In point of fact, he, van Otis, was getting a little impatient, waiting for the call to come. For some time he had been expecting another communication to come through to his Chinese friend, Lee Fong, who had firm Tong connections in Flat Rock.

Van Otis broadened his death's-head smile. It was odd for a Westerner to have that kind of connection with the Chinese Tongs, particularly one that ran a murder service. But he was one man that did. At first, the suspicious leaders of the Tong he was connected to said they desired only pureblood Chinese to carry out their killings, that the white barbarian could not to be trusted, and they summarily rejected Lee Fong's application on his behalf. But Lee Fong was persistent and the Tong leaders in the area gradually began to gain confidence in his judgement. Even more so when they discovered van Otis was no subhuman white killer but an educated man. Finally, they tested him and, much to van Otis's delight, they evidently liked his throat cutting method – the quiet, efficient way he carried out his killings.

Word was sent to the Tong heads in San Francisco. They were reluctant at first but when they were told van Otis would not require remuneration for his services, that really grabbed their attention, as well as their suspicion. However, when he explained that he had private means and that he just wanted the opportunity to rid the world of bad men – he did not mention the intense orgasms he experienced during elimination – they put him on a further six months' trial.

That had been fifteen years ago. Only occasionally unwanted elements reared up in their collaboration. Like the business in Elk Butte a week or so ago; it was a little too near to home for Christian van Otis's comfort. However, the Tong required it so it must be carried out, if he was to remain in their favour. He was warned from the start that refusal would mean his own demise would be the result of demur.

Van Otis continued to smile while congratulating himself on his cleverness. Indeed, who would remotely connect the killing in Elk Butte to that eccentric, slightly odd, Christian van Otis? The man who lived out his solitary life in that big house in Black Cherry Valley, ten miles east of Elk Butte, his only companion a Chinese cripple, Lee Fong? It was too ridiculous for words. And it was a fine house that Papa built in that wonderful Black Cherry Valley, van Otis decided.

Papa bought the valley outright way back in '68, after he made a fortune as a double agent during the Civil War, trading information to both Confederate and Federal. On top of that, he ran a courier service and smuggled in all types of European arms to the Confederacy. What was more, he helped launder money from numerous European organizations that were sympathetic to the South's cause. But here came the clever bit; Papa had the foresight to insist on gold as payment for his services rather than rely on Confederate paper dollars. They weren't worth the paper they were printed on by the time the South capitulated. But the supreme irony was Papa came out of the whole business smelling of roses. He was even decorated for his services to the Federal cause.

As van Otis savoured his cheroot, admiration for Papa filling him as he stared at the wooden, tobacco-smoke-stained ceiling of the Miner's Refuge, his ruminations still savouring the twists and turns in his life.

Papa was sixty years of age by the time the conflict ended. And, clever man that he was, he decided the best thing for him to do was to quietly retire while he was still in front and before the Union got suspicious, if they ever did. He said he worked on the theory: out of sight, out of mind. And thank God Papa picked the wondrous Black Cherry Valley, Montana Territory, as the place to disappear.

There was one black spot, though. Mama claimed she liked Black Cherry Valley, and the splendid house Papa built for her in these wonderful Montana hills. But being a youth sensitive to the true feelings of people, van Otis suspected Mama was saying that only to please Papa . . . that she didn't really like it at all. And that alarmed him, for he loved Black Cherry Valley, loved Montana, the vast solitude of the place, the big skies that seemed to be endless; the fragrant pine forests; the rolling grasslands; he even liked the rocky scrublands. Most of all, he loved the sunsets that flamed red and gold above the far majestic Rockies, towering in the far distance.

81

And here came the final bitter irony in his life. Papa was destined never to fully enjoy his retirement. After seven years he died of a cancer that wasted him away and would have caused him terrible pain had not Lee Fong kept him well supplied with opium, an overdose of which ultimately killed him. It should not have happened to such a fine man, van Otis mourned. He swallowed on the lump that now felt as though it was restricting his throat. Even though he was in this very public place, the Miner's Refuge, he wept quietly, not heeding the hot tears rolling down his sallow cheeks. They did not embarrass him. Most in here were locals, he knew, familiar with his eccentric, harmless even foppish ways. He wanted it to be that way.

But when Papa died, the worst happened, just as he anticipated. Mama wanted to go back to Holland. She hated Black Cherry Valley. She admitted she lied to Papa, that she had always secretly had the desire to go back to her place of birth. She hated America, she said. It was too big, too brash, too hurly-burly for her. She loved the calm, gentle pace of her homeland. She craved to see the canals, the windmills, the fields of tulips in April, longed to skate on the waterways in the cold winters. She wanted to talk and laugh with people that were not constantly driven by the need to achieve, the restless desire to seek virgin land and new opportunities. She wanted go out on to streets and speak her mother tongue . . . not only when she was in the house as she did here in America, but always. Most of all, she was frightened by the intense, raucous energy of the New World, she said.

Finally bored with his morbid thoughts, van Otis got up off the chair and stepped out of the saloon and into the clear descending night. Sitting on the padded leather of the two-seat buggy he'd parked outside earlier, he clicked to the horse in the shafts, flipped the reins and moved out of town along the little-used trail into the hills and towards Black Cherry Valley. However, as he rode dark resentment crowded in like a devil's cloak. Why did Mama lie to Papa all those years, saying she loved America? She left him no choice but to kill her. He did not want to go to Holland; what was in the Netherlands for a man like Christian van Otis? He was a product of the New World. Here was his home.

But he was gentle with her. He certainly did not perform a messy throat-slitting job on her. That method came later when he became really addicted to killing. No, he wanted Mama's death to be dignified, as peaceful as possible.

Lee Fong came up with the answer, though he looked surprised by the request when van Otis made it. He said he knew of an ancient oriental poison. He could quickly get delivery of the stuff if that was what his illustrious American friend truly wanted. It left no trace and induced symptoms similar to influenza. And it did. The Elk Butte doctors did their best to keep Mama alive but she died peacefully in bed a week later, of pneumonia, they said.

Van Otis grinned now. *Sure she did.*

No one suspected foul play. There was a large

turn-out for the funeral. Everyone was enormously sympathetic. Papa and Mama did have a lot of friends in the area. Folks said her death was truly tragic, so soon after his Papa's demise. However, what was so fascinating to van Otis was the ease of Mama's killing and the thrill it gave him, the intense feeling of power and dominance it imbued in him. It was almost like being God, this power over life and death.

Now here he was all these years later, a highly efficient assassin. A man who loved his work while maintaining the illusion he was a harmless eccentric living in his big valley with only the intensely faithful Lee Fong to keep him company.

As for Lee Fong's friendship, that was easy. He was just turned sixteen when it began. He was returning home in disgrace after being expelled from Harvard. He chanced to find the Chinaman by the trail, beaten up and dying. The cold that night was extreme, he remembered. He wrapped Lee Fong up as best he could and carried him home. Papa, for all his history, was a humane man and when he saw the state of Lee Fong he brought in the Elk Butte doctor. The doctor set Lee Fong's broken arm and leg and stitched the many gashes in his face and body. His expulsion seemed to have been forgotten in Papa's rush to do something to aid the man.

For three nights Lee Fong tossed, sweated and shivered, then his fever broke. But the best was yet to come. While Lee Fong was recovering, van Otis, intensely interested in him now, talked to him. Lee

Fong did have a good command of English. Lee Fong spoke of his adventures in his native China and then the long and terrible voyage to America in cruelly cramped conditions.

He talked about helping to build the Central Pacific Railroad, ultimately to join up with the Union Pacific Railroad at Promontory Point, Utah, in 1869. Many died in the terrible conditions they were subject to, he claimed, particularly during the winter of '67, when they laid track and tunnelled across the Sierra Nevada range. He talked about his humiliation when he and his countrymen were kept out of the picture when the photographs were taken of the golden spike being driven in at Promontory Point, done amid much backslapping and cheering and the discharge of many guns. Lee Fong paused here and looked at him with still-bruised eyes. He added wistfully: even the Redmen, who did the white man no favours during that tremendous drive to the West, were there in the background.

As Lee Fong got stronger he said he had many more tales to tell and van Otis begged his Papa to allow him to stay. Though he was still in disgrace at being expelled, his Papa finally agreed; said he needed a wise head to calm him down and he thought Lee Fong would be the man to do it. Papa had no hang-ups about race and culture, but van Otis was to learn Papa's judgement was a little out regarding Lee Fong. He was an assassin back in China, the Chinaman revealed later, prompting van Otis to reveal his own deadly instincts. Lee Fong said he would have been a killer again; only now he was all broken up and unable to do it any more. Nevertheless, it all worked out fine in the end, decided van Otis. Lee Fong introducing him to the Tong, of which he was already a life-long member. Lee Fong never did explain who left him for dead. Van Otis stared at the myriad stars above him. Indeed, whoever was looking after him in that other life was sure doing a good job.

By the time van Otis got to the house it was dark and the wind was keen as it hissed through the black pines. Lee Fong met him at the door with hot coffee and then dealt with the horse and buggy.

Supper over, van Otis now sat to the side of the big log fire in his red Chesterfield armchair, French brandy in hand and staring reflectively into the flames. Lee Fong whispered into the room on his Chinese pumps and bowed.

'Contlact come.'

Van Otis looked up at the small, pigtailed Chinaman. He narrowed his eyelids. Lee Fong must have heard from his Tong connections in Flat Rock.

'Bowden?' he said.

'Didn't say. Think it new one, not Bowden.'

Whatever, thought van Otis. It was always good to be working again. And the client would have been thoroughly vetted first. The Tong, if nothing else, was very careful about that. Secret society meant just that . . . secret. There was no room for mistakes. Punishment was violent and final, if there were any.

'Where do I meet this new client?' van Otis said.

'Same place last time, same time, thlee days flom now.'

'Thank you, Lee Fong.'

'Usual fee, cash now when meet; society insist.'

'In the morning, Lee Fong; you know I keep my word.'

'I know. I wait. You want anything else?'

'No, thank you, you can turn in. Goodnight.'

'Goodnight, Honolable One.'

Lee Fong whispered out again and closed the door quietly behind him.

Van Otis swirled the Napoleon brandy, shipped in from France, and looked into the blazing fire.

Well, now.

Was it Mr Jim McKendry for elimination?

Intriguing.

CHAPTER ELEVEN

Jim was on the trail an hour after first light.

As the sun rose the smell of pine became strong and the varied trills of birdsong filled the sunlit morning with fluting sound. He breathed in deeply of the good air. It was a day to savour, to feel good about. Nevertheless, Christian van Otis's oddness still niggled at him like an open sore. The man *was* a freak. He belonged in a sideshow. But the most perplexing thing about him was the bizarre nature of the man's claims to have psychic powers, that he was able to see the future, experience *vibrations*, whatever they were. It was pure bullshit. And it was pure bullshit Jim McKendry might be the next victim.

Even so, van Otis's assertions still gnawed at him. Indeed, they became so insistent they caused a measure of indecision to well up in him. They became strong enough to occasion him to pull rein on the dun and sit motionless for some moments, staring at his back trail, uncertain as to whether he should go back to Elk Butte and ask Marshal Rimmer what he knew about Christian van Otis.

Questions like, did he know where the freak lived? Did he know what troupe of players he belonged to, if he trod the boards? Questions like that. But after a couple of minutes considering the merits and demerits of his plan, he dismissed it as a waste of time. Van Otis was an oddball, he concluded, a sideshow aberration toting for ticket sales, even though he claimed to be otherwise. Yeah, the idea of Jim McKendry going back to Elk Butte to ask Rimmer about van Otis was not going to be worth the time spent. As for van Otis knowing so much about Pa's killer . . . he must have read some of the wild, speculative stories put out by the editors of sensation-seeking rags. As far as Jim McKendry was aware, nobody knew what that murdering bastard looked like. Even so, Jim looked broodingly at the blue sky, frustrated all to hell by the whole Goddamned mess.

Three days later, dusty and tired, he rode into Flat Rock and as usual stabled his horse at Henry Baron's place. He knew the horse would be looked after without the need to detail specifics . . . fresh bedding straw, clean water, oats and a good grooming. Henry knew the drill.

Jim weaved through the back alleys now, then strolled across Main Street and stepped up on to the brushed-clean boardwalk before the High Life Hotel.

He clumped across the boards and entered the lobby.

At the desk he dabbed dust-muddied sweat off his brow and ordered a bath before going into the saloon to down two schooners of Lisette's renowned beer, chilled by using ice from her cold cellar in the hills. He had to concede; Lisette sure knew how to run a stylish house. Considering that, he came round once more to the speculation: what did the beautiful Lisette Simon see in range-rough Jim McKendry? However, whatever the attraction was, he was not about to complain. Or was his leaving of her six days ago the last straw for Lisette?

He had been treating her badly of late.

He was reading the four-page *Flat Rock Gazette* in one of the comfortable padded leather armchairs spread around the lounge when Lisette Simon, dressed in smooth green satin that clung to her figure like shimmering water, came elegantly down the staircase. She gave the impression she was one of those European queens a man saw in the Eastern magazines that occasionally found their way into Flat Rock – usually brought in by some drummer from back East. Lisette came straight up to him. She had the usual enigmatic smile on her full lips, which promised plenty but was always selective. She cocked an inquisitive, if slightly amused eyebrow.

'Well now . . . back from your travels, lover?'

Catching the hint of cynicism that was there, he rustled the newspaper and gazed up at her. 'Whatever gave you that idea, doll? Jesus, I thought I was still in the saddle and on the way in!'

She winced. 'Ouch. I walked right into that. And from that I take it you didn't catch him. Well, that's real hard potatoes.'

Jim sobered his look. 'Are you here to mock, Lisette? If you are, I'm not in the mood for it right now. I'm hot, I'm tired and the bath I ordered is late.'

'Dearie me.' She swayed her hips. 'Well, maybe I was mocking a little.' She studied him for moments with those blue eyes of hers then she said, 'So, I guess I'd better tell you why I am . . . mocking you, that is. After you left the other day I got to thinking, wouldn't it have been a great idea on your part to use that modem contraption they have down at the telegraph office instead of rubbing your big ass raw riding all the way to Elk Butte.'

Jim glared. Sometimes this lady could be one sarcastic bitch!

She tapped her very kissable red lips with a manicured finger then smiled maliciously. 'If you had, my calculation is you would have saved yourself a round trip of near on two hundred miles. How about that?'

Sourly, he stared at her. 'You're good at maths, too, huh?' He rattled the newssheet a third time in order to express his heightening irritation, even though he knew damn well she was right. He had been a damned fool. He could have used the telegraph. Then the idea hit him like a lightning strike. He stared at her for moments before he put down the rag, got up, kissed her lightly on the cheek and said, 'D'you want to know something, sweetheart? Besides being the most beautiful lady in the whole wide world, you're a real smart gal to boot.'

She raised an amused, pencilled eyebrow. 'Gee, you've finally noticed!'

He grinned. 'Hell, no, not really; I just said it to make you feel good.'

He evaded her swinging right hand that aimed to smack him firmly on the right cheek, turned and paced across the lounge.

'Son of a bitch!' she yelled after him.

Still grinning, he waved a hand. 'Bye for now, sweetheart.'

He was near the door when the deskman called, 'Hey, Jim, how about that bath you ordered?'

McKendry turned. 'Put it on hold, Charlie.'

'Have it brought up to my room,' Lisette said. She turned and stared at him invitingly. 'How does that sound, lover?'

Jim broadened his grin and said, 'Hate to say it but you're full of good ideas today, my blooming prairie rose.'

She lifted her chin enquiringly. 'Only today?'

He continued smiling. 'Don't get carried away, my sweet. See you in ten minutes.'

Her reply battered his back as he went out of the door.

'Go to hell, damn you!'

'Been there. It ain't nice.'

At the telegraph office Jim cabled Marshal Rimmer. While he waited for a reply he went back to share his bath with Lisette. At least there were a few bright clouds on his dark horizon.

CHAPTER TWELVE

Meanwhile, van Otis arrived at Santee Creek an hour before the appointment time set last time by Callum Bowden. He did not see any reason to alter the routine. He dismounted and sat in the shade of a big cottonwood and lighted an expensive cheroot. He waited. Two o'clock in the afternoon, a rider came down the narrow wooded valley the stream had carved out of the rock over millennia and stopped before him and looked down at him. Van Otis was more than a little surprised by what he saw. He said, 'Well, well.'

The rider said, without preamble, 'The requirement is Callum Bowden.'

Van Otis stared. '*Requirement?*' He formed a smile. 'Why, that is a splendid word. I like it, but . . . Callum Bowden? I thought perhaps it would be the new owner of the Rafter M that needed removing.'

'Then you thought wrong, didn't you.' It was a statement.

Van Otis said, 'Apparently.'

The new client said, 'The fee, I believe, is one thousand dollars.'

Van Otis raised a black, kidskin-gloved hand. With it he rubbed his chisel chin, as if pondering on the matter of remuneration. After moments he said, 'Ordinarily, yes, but in view of this new situation a slight adjustment will have to be made, the target being Bowden. I think two thousand would be more appropriate.'

Tightness came to the lips of the rider. 'What's so special about him?'

'He is a valued customer, with potentially more contracts in the offing. A man does not lightly cut off the hand that feeds him.'

'Fifteen hundred.'

'So now we need to barter over your, er, *requirement?*' Van Otis smiled. 'Somehow, I find that obscene, but nevertheless charming.'

The rider stared at him. 'Coming from you, a killer, that's rich.'

Van Otis spread his arms and said, smiling, 'I perform a service. If you think about it deeply enough you will find, at the end of the day, that you are the real killer, not me.'

The rider sat motionless for moments, looking at him and then shrugged. 'See it how you will. Fifteen hundred is my final figure.'

'Seventeen hundred.'

'Sixteen.' The rider fumbled in the long saddle coat pocket, lifted out a wad of notes, counted out eight hundred dollars and offered them. 'Down payment; take it or leave it.'

Van Otis, faintly surprised, smiled and said, 'Nice to see you come prepared. I find that refreshing and impressive, and on the basis of that we have a deal.'

He got up from resting against the tree and paced forward and took the money but the rider withheld it.

'When and how?'

'Can you get the *requirement* into town?' van Otis said. He enjoyed the emphasis he put on the word. 'I will need to have him in a situation similar to last time; a room at the High Life Hotel, two days from now. Overnight stay, of course.'

The client handed over the money. 'I'll do my best.'

Van Otis said, 'You'll have to do better than that.' His dark stare was soulless as he searched the two blue eyes staring back at him, clearly loathing him. He rather liked that. However, he prided himself on being a perfectionist. The conditions needed to be right. There could be no room for error.

The rider paused a moment then said, 'Very well, two days from now, I'll contact you. The usual channel.'

Van Otis bowed extravagantly, with a sweep of his right hand and said, 'It is always a pleasure to do business with one who knows their mind. Have a pleasant journey home.'

The client stared at him and spat on the ground in contempt, but van Otis continued to smile as he put away the eight hundred dollars. The client did not seem to realize that the need for disdain lay with Christian van Otis, not the other way round. Even better, Lee Fong and his associates would be well pleased with this new fee he had just negotiated.

No doubt about that.

CHAPTER THIRTEEN

'Telegram for you, Jim.'

It was the deskman, Charlie. Towel wrapped around his waist, McKendry answered the tap on the door of Lisette's suite, which smelled heavily of perfume. He took the folded piece of paper Charlie poked at him and undid it. It read:

Marshal's office, Elk Butte
McKendry. Re. van Otis. Harmless eccentric.
Forget him.
Rimmer.

McKendry tightened his lips. He was disappointed. Why, he didn't know, he just had these suspicions about van Otis. They would not go away. Indeed, van Otis was not such a dumb ass if he could keep getting away with murder. That's if he was proved to be a killer. Plain fact was, Jim McKendry had not a shred of evidence to say that might be the case; it was just a gut feeling. But there was something about that freak that did not sit right with him, and which kept that opinion firmly in place.

He thanked the deskman and promised to drop a tip off at the desk later and closed the door.

He turned. Lisette was now standing naked and dripping by the galvanized steel bath. She was rubbing her lustrous auburn hair with a large white towel. She said, 'By the look of you, lover, your plan, whatever it was, just hit the buffers.'

'It shows, uh?'

'Yes, so—'

'Fellow named Christian van Otis.'

He explained the meeting in Elk Butte. Lisette took the telegram from him and read it. Then she said, 'Harmless eccentric, uh?'

'That's what it says.'

'But you don't believe it.'

'No.'

Jim began towelling his hair and then his finely muscled body. When he was dry, he dressed. That accomplished he said, with a heavy sigh, 'But the truth is, honey, I just don't know what to believe. It's this constant frustration, the dead ends I keep hitting. Most of all the thought of Pa lying there unavenged in his grave. It eats at me like a dog at a bone. It won't let me be.' He beat a big, callused right fist into his hard left palm. 'Dammit, Lisette, I've got to find this killer; I've got to avenge Pa. I'll know no peace until I do.'

Lisette took the sleek green silk dressing gown off the settee behind her and pulled it on. She sighed and came towards him and put her hand on his chest. 'Jim, you must let it go. Your ma's getting really concerned about you.'

McKendry stared at her, puzzled. 'How d'you know? Have you met her? She did not like having your name even mentioned in the house last time Pa and me talked about you. You know, you and me marrying, and all. She wanted me to forget you, look kindly on one of the ranch girls hereabouts even though Pa always liked the idea of you and me pairing up. He said you had guts, style, brains and would be a real asset. But Ma, well, as I say, she wasn't keen. Even so, she did concede that you were a clever and beautiful woman and would be of benefit to any man, except me. She claimed you'd never fit into ranch life. She was of the opinion you would not want to.'

Jim didn't get the answer he expected.

'In that, she may be right,' Lisette said. She sat down on the settee and with a slim, elegant hand patted a place where she wanted him to sit down beside her. When he did she said, 'I might as well tell you, Jim, Your mother came to see me the other day. As you can imagine, I was more than a little surprised. Well, we talked woman's talk for a while but I could tell she was real anxious about something but could not get it out. I finally took the bull by the horns and asked her to explain what she really came about. She looked relieved I had taken the lead. It was like opening of a floodgate. She said she had come to me as a last resort, in the hope I might have some influence over you, that I may be able to persuade you to give up chasing ghosts and get back to the business of dealing with ranch affairs. She said you had become obsessed with finding your pa's killer and everything else was taking a back seat.'

Jim said, 'What did you say?'

'I said I could not do that, that you were your own man.'

'What did she say to that?'

'She sort of pooh-poohed it; said any woman, if she was determined enough, could get her way with her man.'

Lisette's blue eyes now appealed. 'She's a desperate woman, Jim; she's worried sick. She's lost the husband she loved deeply and does not want her only son to be brought home in a pine box, too. And she's not happy with the way things are going out there at the Rafter M; the way the relationship between Betty Lou and Callum is going.

Jim frowned and held up his hand. 'Hold on, she appeared happy enough about things last time I was at the Rafter M. In fact, she seemed to be real content with Callum's handling of things, and the way things were going between Betty Lou and him.'

'How long ago was that?'

'Three weeks, a month maybe.'

Lisette said, 'Things must have changed, Jim.' Jim felt her hand press gently on to his. 'If it's getting to know about fresh news coming in about your pa's killer that's holding you back, I promise you, I'll get whatever news there is out to the Rafter M as soon as it arrives. Meantime, I think you should go back to the ranch. Your ma is real worried, I could tell.'

Jim looked at her long and hard, then he said, 'D'you want to know something, sweetheart?'

She frowned, clearly not knowing what to expect. 'Go ahead, amuse me.'

'Ma does not deserve to have you as a daughter-in-law. *Now* will you marry me?'

She smiled and toyed with a lock of his blond hair and then caressed his right cheek before she said, teasingly, 'I'm not cut out to be a ranch girl.'

'You can learn, dammit.'

'Maybe.' She leaned back, pursed her lips and appraised him with serious eyes. 'But what I really want to know is . . . why did you dress just now? Supper's not for hours yet.'

Jim stared. How could any man refuse an invitation like that! He undid the belt on her bathrobe in order to once more gaze upon the magnificence of her nakedness. Then he said, 'Right now I'm wondering the same thing.'

CHAPTER
FOURTEEN

Six o'clock the next morning. After a huge breakfast of ham and eggs, flapjacks and honey Jim decided, before he headed for the ranch, he should take a look at the stock situation on the Rafter M.

Being the man who inherited the spread, he had come round to finally admitting he should take Ma's pleas on board and accept Lisette's promise to get news to him, if any came in. For sure, he should buckle down to ranch business, even though it hurt like the very devil to put the hunt for Pa's killer on the back burner. If he was going to be brutally honest with himself, the chance of catching Pa's killer was getting less and less by the day. The truth of the matter was he had nothing to go on. And regarding his suspicions about van Otis, he finally decided they were groundless. If the man that killed Pa was also the man who killed van Otis's mother, well, van Otis had every right to ask questions, seek answers, even though he came over as a freak, a circus performer. Why, dammit, Jim McKendry was doing the same thing!

Perhaps the loss of his mother had unhinged van Otis a little, had turned him into – in contradiction to what Jim McKendry's attitudes would undoubtedly have been and were – the harmless eccentric he appeared to be. Indeed, rationally thinking, the possibility of van Otis being the killer of Pa was becoming patently absurd. Jim suspected van Otis was just a damaged man who was trying desperately to find the murderer of his mother, just as Jim McKendry was trying to find his father's killer, but with much more force.

Breakfast over, Jim went back upstairs and said his goodbyes to Lisette, who was still languishing in bed. He got his rested horse from Henry Baron's, got victuals to last three days from Freddie Jackson's store and then headed north.

By late afternoon he was walking his horse at a leisurely pace along the south bank of Santee Creek. Being exposed to a sun glaring out of a pale blue sky all day, riding the almost treeless range, he now found the willows and aspens lining the slowly moving stream made welcome shade.

Santee Creek formed the north border of the McKendry range. As it was twenty miles from the main ranch he was surprised to see Rowdy Jones coming into view around the bend in the valley up ahead. He eased the bay to a stop and waited for the grizzled old wrangler to reach him. Now up close,

Rowdy said, 'By God, Jim, I sure am glad I bumped into you.'

McKendry frowned. 'How so?'

The ex-wrangler's grey stare engaged McKendy's square on. Rowdy looked as though he had something very serious on his mind, enough to cause the oldster to take a deep breath, sigh and say, 'Jim, though it ain't strictly my business, not being family and all, I can't hold back on it any longer.'

Feeling a tad irritated now that Rowdy should be so reluctant, Jim said, 'Spit it out, old timer, your opinion is respected here.'

'It's your ma and Betty Lou,' Rowdy went on, 'they've been real blue these past three weeks. Not only that, we're losing far more stock than is good for us. Dammit, Jim, your pa would be howling to all hell about the situation if the stock loss happened to him. He'd be beating every goddamned bush, ferreting in every goddamned arroyo in order to run down any owlhoot tracks there might be.'

'Reckon he would,' Jim said. He narrowed his eyelids. 'But you've got something other than that on your mind, ain't you? Spit it out.'

'You maybe won't like it and, like I say, it ain't strictly my business.'

'Let's hear it, dammit. I'll judge if it ain't your business.'

'All right.' Rowdy's grey stare was bold, as usual. 'Jim, your ma needs you at home. You've been away far too long. Things are happening at Rafter M, big things, things I can't put my finger on. But I reckon you should be there, ready to deal with them when and if they come to a head.'

Jim waited for some moments, expecting more. But Rowdy appeared to be waiting for him to say something, maybe bat him down for being so forward, so he said, 'What things?'

Rowdy shrugged. 'I don't know, it's just a hunch, a feeling I have.'

Jim nodded. 'Feeling, huh? Well, fact is, Rowdy, I've been told something similar to that already and not too long ago, and they weren't feelings. That is why I'm heading for home right now. I'm just looking over the stock on the way in. And I agree with you we are a few beeves light but it is not a disaster.'

Rowdy stared as if he was amazed. 'A *few?*' he said. 'Dammit, Jim, I figure more'n three hundred head has been taken since your pa's death. That ain't a few to me, by God.'

Jim stared. He said, 'That many? Dammit, what's Callum been doing about it?'

A sneer formed on Rowdy's purple lips. 'Callum? Now there's a damned mystery for you. Goes out for days on end, says he's looking for rustler sign, or Injun sign, but he never finds a damned thing. But when I follow where he's been a week or two later, I usually find horse tracks and more stock missing. When I tell him what I've found he claims he can't understand it and he'll have to check again when he can find the time. Now I find that mighty odd, Jim, and mighty suspicious.'

Jim said, 'Are you saying Callum's taking the

stock?' He frowned. 'Why would he want to do that? He's part of the family.'

Rowdy shrugged and said, 'That's the big question. But as you know he always had a mile-wide chip on his shoulder, the conviction he should have been given a stake in the Rafter M after your pa died. He didn't get it, did he? Your pa writ it in his will that it only came down to Callum when all other McKendrys were dead.'

Jim stared, hard. 'How d'you know that, old timer? That will was supposed to be for family ears only.'

'Because I helped your pa draft that will, way back.' Rowdy's faded but rock-steady grey stare held Jim's keen gaze for a few moments before he went on, 'Jim, though I don't like to say it, I reckon it could be Callum that had your pa killed and now maybe you're the next on his list. I reckon now your pa's dead he wants the whole hog, snout to tail, and don't give a damn how he gets it.'

Jim stared. 'Now you're getting real wild. Callum's a lot of things, but he ain't a killer, or a cheat.'

Scorn touched Rowdy's wrinkled features as he said, 'You reckon, huh? Boy, you don't know much about human nature.'

Jim studied the short, stocky ex-wrangler intently. It was the first time he had heard Rowdy come out with such statements and so emphatically. The ex-wrangler was usually eager to meet any man halfway and always slow to condemn. Jim shook his head, frowned his doubt and said, 'Naw, I'm not buying it, Rowdy. I'll admit Callum can be a damned fool occasionally, but he ain't a killer, nor is he that ambitious.'

Rowdy said, 'You're wrong, boy.'

Jim studied the old-timer. There was a vehement certainty about the old fellow. But he said, 'Naw, still can't believe it. Now, about those beeves we've been losing. Did Callum take any of the boys with him when he went looking for sign?'

Rowdy shook his head. 'Naw. He said he couldn't spare them and he's been cussing more than somewhat about you not being around, putting all the burden of the ranch's affairs on to him.'

'He should let Bat Losey take some strain. I have told him.'

'He don't seem to want to. Bat's real cut up about it.'

Jim nodded and said, 'He's every right to be. Has Callum brought in Larson Rigby regarding the rustling?'

Rowdy shook his head. 'Naw. Like I said, he doesn't think it's serious enough. That was when I told him he was talking through his ass. Boy, did he get mad. He said that if ever he did get to be boss around here, he'd make damned sure there wasn't a job for me on Rafter M.'

Jim said, 'Aw, he was just kidding around, Rowdy. I shouldn't take too much notice of what Callum says.'

Rowdy rocked moodily in the saddle and said, 'He meant it, all right.' Now his face became sober-looking. 'Jim, as you know, I'm Rafter M to the core, have been ever since we lit out from Kinchella Creek more'n twenty years ago. Son, I don't like the way things are going and you need to see to matters real pronto.'

Jim nodded his head. When Rowdy was in this mood he needed to be taken seriously. He said, 'Noted, old-timer. Where's Callum now, d'you know?'

'Gone into town, as usual.' Rowdy leaned forward, his eyelids narrowing. He added, 'D'you know about his drinking, Jim?'

McKendry frowned. 'I know he likes a snort now and again, but don't we all. It's no big deal.'

Rowdy shook his head vigorously. 'Well, it ain't a snort no more with Callum; he's drinking like there's no tomorrow. My guess is he has something gnawing at his guts real bad. But when I ask him what it is he says I'm a nosy old coot and it's none of my damn business. However, the other night he was real liquored up and forlorn. He took me on one side and said he had to tell somebody his troubles.'

Jim said, 'That's not like Callum.'

'No, it ain't, but out it came, anyway. He said he drinks to take away the hurt he still feels when he thinks about your pa's death and the manner of it, the manner more than anything. You know, throat cut and all.' A sneer now came to Rowdy's lips. 'But I reckon it ain't like that at all, it's something that goes a lot deeper. Son, I'll say it again and risk your anger. I reckon Callum had a hand in your pa's killing and now he can't live with the consequences '

Jim shook his head, his disbelief solid. 'Naw, I can't

109

believe it. You're talking crazy, old timer.' He paused and then added, 'That said, Ma and Betty Lou . . . what do they think about Callum's drinking?'

Rowdy said, 'Your ma says, because of the reason he gives, she can understand his drinking in a way, but Betty Lou . . . well, I'm not so sure 'bout her, something's been eating her up real bad these last few weeks and she's got real remote with Callum. It seems she don't want to know him any more, and that's real unusual.'

Rowdy wrinkled his forehead into worry lines. 'Jim, you've got to get it through your head; things at Rafter M are going all to hell. You've got to get back and untangle the whole business before it's too late.'

Jim looked at the crippled old wrangler and found he was beginning to agree, if what he was hearing was true. And it must be. Both Lisette and Rowdy could not be wrong.

Jim looked into the late afternoon sky. 'I guess you were figuring on bedding down at Long Ridge line camp for the night, uh, Rowdy, so far from home base?'

'That was the plan.' Rowdy leaned forward in the saddle and narrowed his wrinkled eyelids. 'But if you want me to ride back to the Rafter M with you, I'm easy with that.'

Jim nodded and gave the oldster a smile. 'Well, I do want you to ride in, but without me. Tell Ma I'm on my way, but first I need to head into town to try and get Callum straightened out and back at the ranch working.'

'Sounds good to me, but you tread easy around Callum, boy,' Rowdy said. 'I've got bad feelings about him.'

With that, Rowdy turned his roan and sent it up the narrow valley towards South Pasture and Rafter M. Jim watched him go. For sure, that old man was worried and now he was.

He pointed his bay toward Flat Rock with the intention of using the short cut through Devil's Gap. He was swiftly coming to the opinion there were serious things to thrash out with Callum and there were serious things wrong at the Rafter M.

Goddamnit, why did you have to get killed, Pa?

CHAPTER FIFTEEN

It was late evening when Jim rode into town. The heat of the day was gone and the night chill was setting in. He tied up the bay before the High Life Hotel and walked into the lounge area. Charlie, on the desk, looked at him over his glasses.

'Howdy, Jim.'

Jim said, 'Callum around, Charlie?'

'Went out 'bout an hour ago.'

'D'you know where?'

'Didn't say, but he was carrying a load of whiskey, that's for sure.'

Jim grunted his answer and went into the saloon, which was off to his right – got to by passing through the thick, tied-back green drapes each side of the open doors. He saw some familiar figures lining the long mahogany bar that sported a huge mirror behind it, as well as a sumptuous painting of a reclining nude. Again he asked if anybody knew where Callum was. Once more, all answers were in the negative, only one offered something to go on.

'Said he was going out to get some air.'

Jim went out, walked west then down Third Street to the Cumberland Saloon. Again he was met with an unenthusiastic reply. He walked north to the Saddleman's Rest. Similar answers. Dammit, where the hell was the son of a bitch?

Heading back to the High Life Hotel he turned the corner on to Main Street, right where Lo Chang's Laundry and Eating House was. Jim was surprised to bump into Christian van Otis coming out of the dimly lit premises, accompanied by a cloud of stream. Van Otis was smoking a long thin cheroot, which stuck out of his pale face like a pencil. Jim noticed, however, that the eccentric, as Marshal Ernest Rimmer up there in Elk Butte had described him, did not seem overenthusiastic about meeting up with Jim McKendry. Nevertheless, van Otis managed to smile his tombstone smile and say in his refined East coast accent, 'Why, Mr McKendry, what an unexpected pleasure.'

'I live here, van Otis,' Jim said, 'and it's me that's surprised. I did not expect to see you in Flat Rock.'

'A little business, sir, and did I not say our mutual friend would likely strike again and right here?'

'Yeah,' Jim said, 'you did. So?'

'*So?*' Van Otis frowned. 'A strange reaction, if I may say so.' He lifted his chisel-shaped chin, his black stare acute, his pale features amber in the street lantern above. 'Surely the answer is obvious? The killer must be here if my psychic powers dictate correctly, and they do. Mr McKendry, did I not

113

mention this man killed my mother? Surely I have as much right to try and track him down as you have. And that is mainly why I am here.'

'He?' McKendry said. 'You figure he's male then . . . using those vibrations of yours again?' Jim did not attempt to hide his sarcasm.

Van Otis smiled tolerantly and said, 'You may mock, Mr McKendry, but surely you don't suspect the killer to be female?'

Jim shrugged, narrowed his eyelids. 'Rule nothing out is my motto.'

Van Otis looked speculatively at him for a long moment then said, 'You think I am a fool, don't you, Mr McKendry?'

'Not a fool, I just find your claims to having psychic abilities and those vibrations you talk about a little hard to swallow. Being a man who has had to face up to what was clear and in front of him all his life, that's a natural reaction, isn't it?'

'You do not think the ability to look into the future is a reality, then?'

'No.'

Van Otis said, 'Well, you do not mince words, Mr McKendry, and I must admit, you are not the first person to give voice to that opinion. I find that a little sad.'

'You do, uh?' Jim said.

'Yes.' Van Otis now sighed and added, 'Well, I am rather tired, Mr McKendry. It has been a long day. I find three days in the saddle gets to be rather tedious, as well as painful.' Van Otis raised brows. 'I usually ride the stage from Elk Butte to here. However, as you must know, it is only a once-a-week service and this business I am about was too urgent to be left.' Van Otis tipped his hat. 'That said, I will now bid you goodnight, sir.'

He strode off up the boardwalk, back as straight as a ramrod.

McKendry stared after him, his thoughts again becoming deeply suspicious, though the reason why they should eluded him. However, the plain fact was those feelings would not go away, despite considering the fellow harmless earlier in the day. There *was* something strange about him, something sinister.

He opened the door and entered Lo Chang's place. A wind-bell was hanging above the door. It tinkled as the top of the door caught it. A tall, fat-faced Chinaman was pressing trousers the other side of the small counter. Jets of steam were hissing from the machine he was using. Lo Chang put the trousers aside, smiled and came to the small counter.

He said, 'You want laundly doing, mister; some eats maybe? How about Chinese massage? Velly good for aches and pains. Maybe you want pletty Chinese lady? One that knows what big white fellows like?'

Lo Chang continued his benign smile.

'None of those things,' Jim said brusquely. 'What did the fellow just gone out want?'

Lo Chang said, 'Van Otis? He do business. I got good business connections. You want good business connection?'

'Not right now.'

'You want eat, then?'

'No. Now, what kind of business does Mr van Otis do?'

'Business ethic; can't tell – velly bad to tell. You want pants plessing?'

'No.'

'Can't do business then. Close do' when go out. Yes?'

McKendry said, 'Suppose I buy me a meal, pay over the odds, will that loosen your tongue?'

'Blibe, uh?' Lo Chang wagged a finger. 'No take blibe, mistah. Lo Chang get into big tlouble if take blibe.' The Chinaman smiled secretly and touched his nose. 'You want other fine Chinese lady maybe? Yes? This Chinese lady velly good to white man with big tlouble; she makes you feel velly good. Help you dleam of lotus. You want to go up to dleamland, mistah? She take you.'

McKendry shook his head vigorously. 'To hell with that.'

'No hell,' said Lo Chang. 'Lotus heaven; use white man's opium.'

Jim slammed the door on the man's coaxing voice and marched up Main Street, the noise of the wind-bell over the door tinkling long after Lo Chang's plea was dead. A slight drizzle began falling. Jim pulled up his coat collar. He made tracks back to the High Life Hotel to collect his bay secured to the tie rail there. He thought about paying Lisette a call, but, tempting though that was, this time he knew he must get back to the Rafter M.

He rode out of town. He cursed the rain that was now wetting him through, cursed because he had nothing to show for his long trip. However, the cussing did not help lighten his black mood one bit. Even so, to hell with van Otis, to hell with Lo Chang and, above all, to hell with Callum Bowden! Let him rot his goddamned liver if that is what he wanted to do!

CHAPTER SIXTEEN

By the time Jim got to Rafter M the rain had stopped and the moon was out. He found the ranch house and the bunkhouse were in darkness. Well, that was not unusual at one o'clock in the morning.

He rode the tired and wet bay into the nearest barn, stalled it and wiped it down with hay. Then he watered it and fed it oats. After that he headed for the ranch house, the mud squelching under his soggy boots. The wind was raw and cold against his face, as it had been all the way home.

Inside, he went to his bedroom and changed into dry clothes and boots. In the kitchen, he saw the stove was built up to last overnight. He opened the draught flap and got it roaring. The stove soon heated up. He set the draught control a quarter open. He put coffee and water in a can and boiled it up. Then he filled his tin mug and sat down to gratefully drink the hot brew. The cold in his bones soon began to thaw.

Minutes later Ma whispered into the kitchen on

soft slippers. She sighed and came to him and wrapped her arms about his massive shoulders. She said, as though a great weight had been lifted from her shoulders, 'Rowdy said you were on your way. Oh, Jim, thank God you've come home. How we need you.'

Betty Lou came to the door. 'Where's Callum? Rowdy said you'd gone to fetch him home.'

There was an odd anxiety in her voice, Jim thought, as though she did not want him home. Was Rowdy right when he said she and Callum seemed to have grown apart lately? Well, Jim McKendry would not weep over that.

He looked into his sister's questioning and troubled blue eyes. He said, 'I didn't find him, though I didn't look too hard. He's a grown man. He'll come home when he's ready, I guess.'

Betty Lou said, 'Yes, yes, he will.' Then she came to him, kissed him on the cheek. 'I'm so glad you've come home, Jim. It's been real bad around here without you.'

Again, Jim found her reaction odd. Callum was the real bright light in her life, always had been. Jim McKendry was just her troublesome, teasing brother though he knew she loved him dearly despite that. He said, 'Is that so, sister? What brought this on? You pleased to see me? I was under the impression Callum was doing a good job here and he was the only one around able to cheer you up.'

Instead of her usual caustic retort Betty Lou stared, clearly hurt, tears filling her eyes. Then the strained lines in her face set hard. 'Damn you, Jim, you can be real cruel when you want to be.'

She ran from the room sobbing, her hands covering her pale face. Jim stared after her, open-mouthed.

Ma turned on him and said, 'There was no call for that, Jim. I reckon she's real worried about Callum going off the rails and she ain't over Pa's dying yet. Have some compassion.'

Jim thought: women! But he said, as if to make a half-assed apology, 'Maybe I was a little harsh.'

Ma stared. 'A little! You were down right rude.'

'Perhaps.' He could rarely handle women when they were in this mood. They seemed to have answers for everything, when, truth be told, they were just nagging. He bent and kissed his mother gently on the forehead. 'I'm tired, Ma. I guess I'll get some sleep.'

As he bent, Ma's hand grabbed his arm and her pleading grey stare found his. 'Have you really come home this time, Jim?'

'I reckon,' he said. 'Come first light I want to take a good look at the situation on the range, boundary to boundary. Guess that'll take me best part of three days, maybe a touch longer. But, yes, I'm home.'

His mother sighed. 'I'm so glad you're beginning to accept the possibility that your pa's killer will never be found.'

Jim found that core of steel inside him harden again, making his reply brittle. 'I'll never accept that, Ma, never.'

He turned and headed for his bedroom.

*

Sun-up, Marshal Larson Rigby came riding into the ranch precincts. Jim was saddling up in preparation to head out on his range inspection. He stopped what he was doing and waited for the lawman to come close. When Larson reached him Jim stared up into the Flat Rock lawman's stem features. He said, not trying to hide the curiosity that was in him, 'What brings you out to Rafter M so early, Larson?'

Rigby compressed his thin lips. His face, Jim noticed, was unusually pale and grave. For moments Rigby fumbled with the horse's reins. There was clearly something on his mind. Finally he said, 'Dammit, Jim, there ain't no easy way to say this, so I'll just come right out with it: Callum's dead, murdered.'

McKendry stared in disbelief, couldn't help repeating, '*Murdered?*'

Rigby nodded. 'It's a carbon copy of your pa's death. That bastard really enjoys his work.'

Jim shook his head, disbelief rampant in him, and he stared hard at the grim-faced marshal. He remained silent for moments and then he said, 'I just can't take this in. What's going on, Larson?'

Rigby scrubbed his bristles with a callused hand. He said, 'That's the question I've been asking myself all the way to here. It just doesn't make any sense at all. Your family have a real fine name these parts. There's no good reason for it.'

Jim screwed up his eyes against the brightness of

121

the early morning sun, a foot or two above the hilly eastern horizon and bursting new-morning light down upon the ranch environs. After moments he said, 'Have you got any leads at all?'

Rigby shook his head. 'Nary a one. It's a carbon copy of the last murder. Jim, that damned butcher is long gone.'

They both heard the harsh, whimpering gasp. They both turned. Ma was standing in the frame of the ranch house door. The bottom of her apron was clasped to her pale face. Her eyes were full of disbelief as she peered over the top of it. She had clearly been listening.

Rigby immediately took off his worn brown Stetson. He said, 'Sarah, I didn't know you were there. I just don't know what to say, I truly don't.'

Ma stared. It seemed she was desperately trying to overcome her sorrow. When she appeared to have gotten hold of herself she said, 'Have you eaten yet, Larson?'

Rigby stared, as if with some amazement, then he coughed, screwed up his hat and shuffled on his worn saddle boots, as if embarrassed. 'Why, no, ma'am; I came here as soon as I knew about Callum. I thought you'd want to know.'

'We do, but a man should not go without his breakfast to do it.' Ma lifted her chin, her face set, as if carved out of alabaster. 'Climb down, Larson, tie up and come in; food's already cooking.'

Rigby flicked an inquiring eye on to Jim, as if he was questioning Sarah McKendry's state of mind at that moment. Jim shrugged, raised brows almost imperceptibly as if to say, 'Beats me, too, but go ahead'. On the strength of that, Rigby said, 'Well, thank you, Sarah. I got to say, the ride has made me more than a little peckish.'

'So, that's settled, then.'

They followed Ma into the kitchen. Rigby sank into one of the six chairs around the long deal table. Jim seated himself in another and Ma placed eggs and fat-back in the skillet on the stove. Bacon soon began to chuckle and spit in the pan. While she was stood over the stove Ma said, apparently composed now, 'What do you intend to do this time, Larson?'

Rigby said, 'Well, it's not quite the same as last time. We've got Edmond Fugère in town. He's French-Canadian – trapper, hunter. He rides in occasionally to relax and tout for business. He's volunteered to go look for sign. Now, if *he* can't find tracks then nobody can.'

Jim said, approvingly, 'Fugère's a good man. He occasionally does work for the Rafter M, keeping predator numbers down.' Then he looked keenly at Rigby. 'How's Lisette Simon taking it? This was the second time murder had been done on her premises.'

Rigby pursed his lips and raised grey brows and said, 'Well, I've no worries on that score. She's a real feisty lady, is Lisette. She'll cope, like she did last time. But you don't need me to tell you that.'

Jim coloured slightly. 'Just asking. You never know.'

Ma said, while turning the sizzling bacon, reproof in her tone, 'You should make an honest woman of her, Jim. I don't approve of what's going on.'

Jim stared at her, a touch of anger firing through him. Nevertheless, he kept calm and said, 'Lisette Simon is about the most honest woman I know, Ma. I'd be obliged if you'd leave it at that for now, things being the way they are.'

But Ma persisted. 'There's two kinds of honest in my book, Jim,' she said. 'The one the Lord recognizes and the one nature does. I'm on the Lord's side, and so should you be. Marry her.'

Jim said, still suppressing his resentment, 'Lisette will decide on that in her own good time. Let it drop. This is not the time.'

His mother began beating the spatula she was turning the bacon with against the edge of the skillet with unnecessary violence, then she said, as if in apology, 'I'm hurting, Jim. Things just ain't the same any more. This is the only way I know of to handle it, doing something, saying something ... keeping busy.'

She turned from the cook range. With the large skillet in her hand she swept four eggs and six rashers of fat-back onto Rigby's plate with the spatula. Then she said, 'You're sitting there like a dog who lost his bone, Larson; get to eating. Bread's on the table; cut what you want.'

Then she put the skillet and spatula down and rushed from the room, her apron bottom held in her right hand and dabbing her eyes.

Both men stared after her. Rigby said, disapproval in his voice, 'You were more than rough there, boy.'

Jim stared, but kept his peace. He would store his wrath for the bastard that caused all this.

CHAPTER SEVENTEEN

Before they got up to leave, Ma came back into the kitchen. Her eyes were red with crying, but she looked herself again, composed and calm. Silently, she began washing the plates. Jim went to her side, gently suggested that it would be pointless Betty Lou and she getting Rowdy to hitch the horse to the buggy and join them on the ride into town. He would make all the necessary arrangements. Then he would send the body back to the ranch for burial, alongside Pa's remains there on the top of Sunrise Hill, half a mile east of the ranch and which gave a view of almost the whole of Rafter M range.

'That'll be fine, Jim,' she said and continued washing the breakfast things, intently scrubbing and scrubbing at them.

Ma would get over things in her own good time, he knew. But what Jim did find odd was Betty Lou staying in her room; she and Callum were so close, or had been.

126

He felt he should go to her. However, he was always so clumsy and inarticulate when dealing with this kind of thing. It was not that he did not feel things, he did, strongly, but he always seemed to do and say the wrong things when called upon to comfort the grieving, particularly family. He felt sure Ma would go through to her as soon as Larson and he were out of the way, if she hadn't already done so just now. Women, he knew, were much better at that kind of thing. Even so, it made him feel like a coward riding away like this without saying something, or just taking her in his arms for a spell to absorb her pain and show he was feeling for her and that he loved her and wanted to protect her.

Outside, he climbed into the saddle. Rigby was already seated and waiting. As they rode past Betty Lou's bedroom, Jim could hear her quietly sobbing. He spurred his horse into a run, angry with his acute sense of frustration and inadequacy. Who and where was that murdering son of a bitch!

After a five minute gallop he slowed the bay down to a fast walk. Larson, puffing and panting, came up alongside him. 'You got it out of your system now, boy?' he said.

Jim snorted, 'Not by a hell's half acre.'

An hour later they rode into Flat Rock and dismounted before the law office. Mal Delaney met them on the boardwalk. Nothing had come out of his investigations, he said. His frustration was clear. Like last time, folks saw nothing, heard nothing. It was plain they'd hit another dead end. Worse was to come. Edmond Fugère, after an hour's thorough search, had found nothing. Mal added that it was a very disgruntled French-Canadian trapper that rode out of Flat Rock an hour ago on his big brown mule, trailing his fully loaded pack donkey behind him. Mal finished, with a heavy sigh, 'That Fugère, he don't like admitting defeat.'

Jim said, with some bitterness, 'What man does?' He turned to Rigby. 'Have any other strangers hit town recently?'

'Edmond Fugère, is all,' said the lawman, 'but he isn't a stranger.' Rigby narrowed his eyelids, his gaze searching. 'If you're thinking what I think you are thinking, Jim, forget it – Fugère is innocent. He was drinking and playing cards in the Cumberland Saloon until the early hours of this morning. After that, according to barman Pop Eye Jake Cameron and several others, he fell into an alcohol-induced sleep under the table around three in the morning and didn't move until somebody woke him for breakfast at seven thirty.'

Jim pursed his lips. 'Anybody else?'

'Not that I know of,' Larson said. 'If there was, he came in real quiet and left the same way. Dammit, Jim, while I don't like blowing trumpets, Mal and me, we don't miss much.'

Jim sighed out his feelings of helplessness and remounted his bay. He looked down and nodded and touched the brim of his hat.

'I'll see you around, gents.'

Rigby held up a delaying hand and said, 'Jim, leave

this to the law. Get back to the ranch. Your ma needs you more than ever now Callum's dead.'

Jim resented Rigby's interference, but he knew it was meant kindly and he said, 'You know I can't do that, Larson.'

'You can try, dammit!' said Larson. 'Sarah's a dear friend of mine. I'm concerned for her.'

Jim's stare was bleak. 'And you think I'm not?'

Rigby stared at him moodily and then waved a hand. 'Dammit, you know what I mean, Jim.'

McKendry felt a softening in him for the family's long-time friend. He said, quietly, 'Larson, that son of a bitch killed my pa, now he's killed my brother by adoption. If it takes me until doomsday, I'll find him.' He touched his hat and looked at the both of them from atop his horse and added, 'And perhaps this time things will be different.' He turned the bay and rode away, tall in the saddle, but not far. First he stopped off at Jedidiah Bartlow's establishment. He viewed Callum's body and made arrangements to have it shipped out to the Rafter M for burial on the family plot, then he stabled his horse at Henry Baron's. After he headed for Lo Chang's place of business, because riding away from Larson and Mal he remembered there was another stranger in town last night . . . Christian van Otis.

As he opened the door the wind-bell over it chimed. He closed the door behind him. The interior was still hot, steamy and gloomy. The smell of soap and Chinese food being cooked made an odd mixture on the moist air.

129

As usual, Lo Chang was behind his ironing board, working. He grinned when he entered. He came to the counter. 'You change mind, huh, mistah? You want nice, soft Chinese lady aftah all?'

McKendry said, 'Where's van Otis, Lo Chang?'

The Chinaman raised dark brows. 'Van Otis? He gone. He done business. He don't stay aftah done business.'

'Gone . . . where? Back to Elk Butte?'

'He no say. He nevah say. He just go when business done.'

'I think you're lying.'

'Lo Chang no lie. Why Lo Chang lie?'

Anger began to build up in McKendry. Every damned turn he was met with a wall of evasion. Didn't anybody know anything in this town, or any other goddamned town? He grabbed the Chinaman by the lapels of his cheap black suit, pulled him close and said, 'Mister, get this straight . . . I'll beat the truth out of you if you don't come out with some answers real quick.'

Lo Chang's oriental eyes grew alarmed. He raised his hands and shrieked, 'No beat, Lo Chang have nothing to tell. Van Otis come, he do business, he go. Why he tell lowly Lo Chang what he do?'

Jim shook him. 'What sort of business, dammit?' He drew back his right fist. 'I got to know, you hear me?'

However, McKendry's gut went Artic cold when he saw Lo Chang's gaze slide past his shoulder and turn to a look of horror. He cried, 'No kill white pe'son!

130

No kill any white pe'son here! Velly bad for Chinese people to kill white pe'son; velly bad for business.'

McKendry released Lo Chang and turned, his hand streaking for his Colt .45. But the warning that came to him from behind was terse and full of intent. 'You dlaw gun, we kill.'

McKendry froze his clawed hand above the butt of his Colt. He finished the rest of his turn carefully. He saw two Chinamen were immediately behind him; a third was leaning against the door, clearly to prevent anyone entering, or leaving. The two men directly behind him were holding meat cleavers in raised positions, inches from his head. He throat went very dry.

Lo Chang came around the counter. He said, 'You go now, McKendly. Lo Chang don't want double. No Chinee want double with 'Melican.'

Jim stared. 'You know my name?'

'Everybody know McKendly name.'

Jim did not feel frustration or helplessness very often. Right now he was feeling both in full measure. Even an idiot should know that one bad move, at this moment and in these circumstances, could be the last one they ever made. He had heard about the Tongs, the Chinese secret societies, particularly the ones on the west coast, and the things they do.

Reluctantly, he raised his hands. 'No trouble.'

Lo Chang bowed. 'McKendly is velly sensible man. Come any time. Lo Chang find McKendly velly special Chinese lady, velly good opium pipe; dleamland is waiting for McKendly.' Then his smile

131

vanished, became sinister, and he waved a curt hand at the three Chinese to let him pass.

They parted.

On stiff legs Jim began to walk to the door. He did not like to climb down before any man; however, there was a lot to be said for the use of a little discretion on occasion. The Chinaman on the door moved aside, bowed and opened it. 'Goodbye, McKendly. Lo Chang always open to do business. You tell evelybody. Always get gleat deal off honoulable Lo Chang.'

Jim stared hard into dark expressionless Chinese eyes before he stepped out on to the boardwalk and into bright noon sunlight. Once there he breathed a little easier. The mud on the street, left from last night's rain, was now dry and the steam it raised was gone to leave hot, moist heat that seemed to stick to his face like wet paper. For a few moments he toyed with the idea of getting Larson Rigby and Mal Delaney to join him in dealing with Lo Chang and his staff . . . drag the bastards out and make them talk . . . but he knew it would be to no avail. He was certain Lo Chang feared something far more deadly than the Flat Rock law and Jim McKendry – the power and far-reaching arm of the Chinese secret societies. If the stories Jim had heard were true, one step out of line and Lo Chang and his boys would be dog meat and real quick. If they were members, that is. He did not know, but he strongly suspected they might be. He strode down the boardwalk. His frustration was so strong he did not hear the kind words of condolence that were coming to him from people he passed, nor did he see the looks of puzzlement, or resentment on some faces as he ignored them. His mind was totally focused on finding van Otis. That man must fit into this mess somewhere. It was a gut feeling, though he did not have anything substantial to back it up, but it was a strong emotion, nevertheless. For one thing, van Otis was in town last night. He said he had rode in to do business. What sort of business? Murder? Why not? The question now was, had he left town yet?

He headed for Henry Baron's livery barn to ask about horses and riders. Henry said van Otis picked up his horse ten o'clock last evening. Jim frowned. Riding at night; a man that wasn't used to riding? And what was the rush? Surely morning would have done just as well.

New energy filled Jim. He soon became convinced another trip to Elk Butte would be more than beneficial. He needed to have another talk with Marshal Rimmer, needed to have another talk with Christian van Otis.

Just needed to get something rolling, dammit!

CHAPTER EIGHTEEN

Grim-faced and cold-eyed, an hour later Jim rode out of Flat Rock and hit the Wells Fargo trail to Elk Butte.

But right about this time van Otis found it pleasant sitting under the cottonwoods by Santee Creek, his horse contentedly grazing on the lush grass. The early afternoon sun was warm and pleasing on his tall, thin frame. At his ease, he smoked his cheroot elegantly as he watched his client come down the narrow valley towards him.

Once more, the river was in spate and was full of brown silt, no doubt due to the rain the previous night. And van Otis, being a man who looked for meaning in everything, found the phenomenon odd, even disconcerting, because the last time he did business in this area it rained heavily. He decided – as he watched his client come nearer – it would be perfectly reasonable to consult his books when he returned home, just in case there was any significance to the odd circumstance. As the rider eased the mount to a halt before him, van Otis flicked his cheroot into the river and climbed to his feet.

'Are you alone?' he said.

'Yes.'

Van Otis smiled and held out his hand. 'Eight hundred dollars, I believe, you owe me. The balance on account?'

He sensed the rider was edgy, certainly not happy, and he felt tautness creep into him because of it. A sixth sense was telling him the client was building up to something that might prove unpleasant.

When the client did not reply immediately, he made a movement as if to adjust his shirt cuff but undid the leather clasp over his gutting knife hilt instead. He said, 'Are you satisfied with my work?'

The rider still sat silently staring at him and van Otis felt his whole body go tense, animal alert.

'Lost your tongue?' he said. He was smiling now.

A look of madness came into his client's eyes. 'Did you have to kill him in that awful way?'

Van Otis relaxed slightly and shrugged. 'The dead are dead. Does it matter how they die? Let me remind you, you bought a killing and I have carried it out. If you want somebody to blame, blame yourself.' He pushed out a hand again. 'Eight hundred dollars, please.'

The client suddenly gave out with a wild cry. 'You are an animal!'

The client was wearing a long saddle coat and was fumbling in the right patch pocket . . . for a gun, or for money, van Otis wondered? He did not wait to find out. With the speed of a striking rattler van Otis drew his knife and flipped the blade expertly. It travelled fast and true and hit the client full in the chest. Blood blossomed like a huge red rose.

The client gasped, went as loose as a rag doll and fell off the horse to hit the ground with a soapy thud. But still the client continued to fumble.

Van Otis stepped forward. He twisted the blade and pulled it out of the client's chest. He slit the client's throat, looking into the client's terrified eyes as he did it. When the client was dead he fumbled in the pocket the client had been reaching for. He found a loaded Remington derringer. In another pocket he found eight hundred dollars in hundred dollar bills. Smiling, he pocketed the money and left the client's body where it lay. He mounted and rode away.

He decided he needed rest and recuperation, and he resolved to do something about that when he got back to Black Cherry Valley: ramble through the hills, maybe hunt for deer, though he was usually loath to kill them. More often than not he just lay back and admired the grace and exquisiteness of such beautiful creatures.

The tedious side of these things Lee Fong would deal with. He would attend to all the details regarding paying off the Tong. After that, maybe he would take his Chinese friend off for a much-needed holiday. Perhaps they would visit Philadelphia or New Orleans or New York, or maybe they would travel down to San Francisco for a real whirl.

Wherever the whim would take them. Perhaps he would be able to drum up some business as well, make a few deals. Like his Papa, he was good at making money and had good connections.

CHAPTER NINETEEN

Noon three days on, Jim was in Elk Butte. He was sitting in the hardback chair in Marshal Rimmer's office. Even though he was dusty, trail worn and tired, he hadn't even bothered to stop off at a hotel to clean up before coming here, so keen was he to get *something* moving.

He gave Rimmer the details of Callum's death and his suspicions regarding Christian van Otis. Rimmer immediately looked dubious and shook his head. 'I don't want to pour oil on your assumptions, McKendry, but you're barking up the wrong tree there. Van Otis is a pussy cat; he wouldn't hurt a fly.'

'He was in Flat Rock when Callum was killed.'

'Still don't mean a thing,' Rimmer said, toying with the pen in his hand. 'He moves around all the time. Goddamnit, he's a businessman. He does deals.' The lawman sighed. 'Look, though I don't like to rule anything out, I find it highly unlikely van Otis is the killer. I would be on to him if he were. No, I figure that throat job we had here was a copy-cat killing, like I said at the time. If it were van Otis, he wouldn't soil his own nest, he's too smart for that.' Then Rimmer looked at Jim for some moments as if he was having second thoughts, or saw something in Jim's earnestness that was changing his mind. Then he said, 'You're real set on this, ain't you, McKendry?'

'Yes, I am.'

Rimmer twirled his pen some more and then sighed. 'OK, I'll give you the route to his house. But I warn you, he's a very private man and he won't like the intrusion.'

Jim said, 'D'you think I'm bothered about that?'

Rimmer's stare was level, concentrated, then he said quietly, 'McKendry, I want that murdering bastard brought to justice just as much as you do; I just don't think it's van Otis, that's all. But if I'm proved wrong, I won't whine about it. That throat job was a real vicious killing. Nevertheless, if you do come up with something, come back to this office. Don't take the law into your own hands.'

Jim said, 'That might not be so easy.'

Rimmer said, 'Never said it would be, but that is what I require you to do.'

Jim said, 'Rimmer, I won't promise a thing. If it does turn out van Otis is the killer and he comes at me with that damned knife he uses, he'll be a dead man.'

Rimmer shrugged. 'We'll deal with that when we get to it. But right now I still think you're barking up the wrong tree.'

'We'll see about that.'

'We will,' Rimmer said.

Jim went through the office door, closing it behind him.

He followed the little-used trail Rimmer directed him to. It wound through low hills. Black Cherry Valley, he found, was a beautiful place, woods, grassland and game in abundance. The massive, well-built grey stone ranch-style house was at the head of the valley. It was far too big for one man, thought McKendry, if there *was* only one man.

He rode straight up to the long, white-painted wooden gallery and climbed down at the hitch rail before it. He mounted the two steps and knocked on the solid oak door. He waited, knocked again. After a couple of what seemed stretched out minutes a high-pitched call came from inside.

'Go away. No wanted.'

McKendry frowned. The accent. Another Chinaman?

He said, 'I need to talk with Mr van Otis.'

'Not here; go away.'

McKendry decided he had not travelled one hundred or more miles to be turned back that easy. Maybe van Otis was not at home, but he'd damn well search the house to make sure he wasn't.

'When will he be home?'

'Not know. Why I know? Me only selvant; he come, he go, he no tell Lee Fong where he go.'

'What if I kick the damned door down?' McKendry said, his anger beginning burn inside him.

140

'You no kick,' Lee Fong said, his voice rising. 'You pay if kick down. Lawman Limmer he fix you good if you kick do' down.'

McKendry hammered on the door with the butt of his Colt. 'Dammit, man; open up, you hear me?'

'Go away.'

The voice from behind, which Jim instantly identified as belonging to van Otis, said, 'Really, such aggression, Mr McKendry. Is it necessary? Even so, I must apologize for Lee Fong's rudeness. However, being a loyal employee he is very protective of my privacy, and my property. I prize that and would not think of admonishing him for it. Now, sir, how can I help you?'

Jim turned. Van Otis was sitting his hard-ridden horse about a dozen yards behind him. His all-black dress was dusty and trail-worn. There were also dark stains down the front of the suit and on the sleeves, but hardly distinguishable against the black material. Could be anything, Jim thought; it was hardly an issue.

'You move quiet, van Otis,' he said.

'Yes, I do. You want to speak with me?'

'That's the general idea.'

'In what capacity?'

'A few things I want to clear up.'

Van Otis raised dark brows; his face became serious. 'I see. Well, if you have news of the whereabouts of the killer we both want caught that will be splendid. But first you must excuse me; I have had a long and tedious ride and I am badly in need

141

of a bath and a change of clothes. Nevertheless, you must stay for supper now you are here. Lee Fong is an excellent cook. Indeed, it looks as though you have also spent long hours in the saddle recently yourself. If that is the case I cordially invite you to stay the night. It would be very churlish of me if I didn't. Elk Butte is at least a ten mile ride and the trail must still be strange to you.'

McKendry just did not know what to make of this odd, gaunt man with the skull-like looks. Van Otis still looked as though he had just stepped out of a melodrama, a caricature of the dastardly villain portrayed in any stage play worth its salt. As for his psychic abilities and sensing vibrations as he calls them, it was still pure bunkum as far as Jim McKendry was concerned. However, he was tired, he was hungry and he acutely needed to get to grips with this man, needed to bear down on him, get to know what really went on in that mind of his, and if he really is the killer or just the passive eccentric people around here believe he is.

He said, 'Van Otis, that's an invitation I can't refuse.'

Van Otis smiled his tombstone smile. 'Good, that's settled, then.'

He raised his voice. 'Open up, Lee Fong, Mr McKendry will be our guest for the night.'

The stout door swung open to reveal a small Chinaman. His round, Oriental face, Jim noticed, was badly scarred, ugly even. Lee Fong came out on to the long gallery. He walked across it with a

142

pronounced limp, but the disability did not seem to affect his movements overmuch. The gallery, Jim observed, was furnished with two cane tables, six cane chairs; gaudy cushions were placed tidily on them. A hammock was swinging in the light afternoon breeze at the far end.

Van Otis climbed down from his horse. Clearly, he was tired and stiff from his long ride. Jim narrowed his eyelids. Long ride? Henry Baron, stable owner back in Flat Rock, said van Otis picked up his horse around ten o'clock at night, nigh on four days ago. Van Otis should have been back home long before now. Could he have stopped off somewhere to do a little more killing?

Van Otis was saying, 'Stable the horses, Lee Fong, and then prepare my bath and lay out a clean suit.' He plucked at his dirty, stained clothes. 'Oh! And burn these rags, will you?'

Lee Fong stared. 'No wash, no keep?'

'No. Dispose of them.'

The Chinaman took the horses by the bridles. McKendry noticed the stables were one hundred yards to the left and to the rear of this fine building. They, too, were built of grey stone, like the ranch house.

'I saw you were admiring the house, Mr McKendry,' Van Otis said. 'My father built it for my mother, but unfortunately he died soon after it was completed. Sadly, Mother did not like the house, did not like America in fact – unlike Father, who loved the rip-roaring drama of this great country. But she

143

was obedient to Papa's wishes and bore the necessity of staying gracefully, while he was alive. But as soon as he died she said she wanted to return to Holland. That is in Europe, by the way. It was the place of her birth, my father's, too.' Van Otis touched his lips with a thoughtful finger. 'Oh! And I'm sure I mentioned in our previous conversations that it was our mutual enemy that killed my mother and thus ruined her desire to return to her homeland?'

Jim nodded. 'Yes, you did.'

Van Otis nodded his satisfaction. 'Ah! Good. Now, do you come with news of the murderer?'

'I have a few ideas about him,' Jim said.

Van Otis stared for moments and then said, 'Really? Well, they will be interesting to know, but can it wait until dinner? As I said, I'm dirty, tired and definitely in need a bath and a change of clothes.'

'I guess it will make for interesting conversation,' Jim said.

Van Otis beamed, as if delighted he was bringing news. 'Indeed, it will. I cannot wait for dinner to come.'

Jim ran his narrow gaze over van Otis's travel-stained attire, particularly the dark marks, lightened by dust, on the sleeves and down the front of the jacket and trousers of the black suit. It was as though Van Otis had been splashed with some dark, viscous substance. Blood? Cutting a man's throat must be a messy business and very likely left stains. However, this was pure speculation and he did not normally have much time for guesswork; facts were what he

144

usually worked on. Nevertheless, the abstract notion was worth taking note of.

He followed van Otis into the house. The fine interior stretched before him. Smooth plastered walls, antlers and moose heads and pictures mounted on all of them. The room van Otis led him into was large and lushly furnished. A huge log fire burned and snapped in the immense open fireplace. Horse brasses hung down the two grey stone side pillars each side of it. Ornaments of several kinds and a large ormolu clock were lined up on the marble mantelshelf.

Van Otis fondled one of the brasses. 'English,' he said, 'an indulgence of my father. The clock is French.' He turned and stared at Jim and added pensively, 'He was a man I dearly loved, Mr McKendry. He is still greatly missed.' He waved to the one of the armchairs. 'But, please, be seated; make yourself at home. A drink?'

'Have you bourbon?'

'Of course. Kentucky's finest.'

A variety of named decanters stood on a silver tray on a large polished table near the big window. Van Otis picked one up and poured the drink into a cut-glass tumbler. When he passed it to McKendry he said, 'I will leave you now.' He waved a hand to another table nearby. 'There are eastern magazines, the *Elk Butte Courier*, books in the bookcase.' He also flapped a hand toward the shelves full of books that stood floor to ceiling against the far wall.

'Are you a reader, Mr McKendry?'

'Can't say that I am.' Jim sipped the smooth bourbon.

'That is a pity. Reading is one of the great pleasures in life . . . in my opinion, of course.'

'Sure. But not mine particularly.'

Lee Fong came to the door and bowed. 'Bath leady.'

Van Otis smiled to express his delight. 'Good.' He beamed at Jim. 'So, I will leave you to it, Mr McKendry. Please, help yourself to another drink if you feel the need for one.'

'Will do,' Jim said.

He eased back against the plush upholstery of the chair and relaxed, but after twenty minutes he got up, got himself another drink and browsed along the rows of leather-bound books. The authors' names on the bindings facing him meant little. Dickens, Brontë, Mark Twain, Fennimore Cooper, dozens more, then came three volumes in fine brown leather. On them, embossed in gold leaf, were the titles *My Diaries*. Jim narrowed his eyelids. Well now . . . people sometimes put a lot of secrets into their diaries, if they are van Otis's, that is.

He was about to lift one down when van Otis entered the room, spruce and clean but still in black. The suit was of fine material and fitted him like a glove. The one relief feature was the grey cravat, which looked to be made of silk and was held in place by a diamond pin. Another thing, which was slightly obnoxious to McKendry, was that van Otis reeked of that woman's stuff they call cologne.

As soon as he entered, van Otis said, 'Again I am remiss, Mr McKendry. You look as though you could do with freshening up yourself. Dinner will be another hour so I have taken the liberty of having Lee Fong prepare a bath for you. Will that be all right?'

Jim stared into those black eyes, which were studying him intently. For sure, he'd never run into a dude like this one before.

He said, 'Sounds just the ticket.'

'Good, but of course, I cannot offer you a change of clothes. For one thing, we have nothing your size. You are rather a large man, Mr McKendry.'

'The bath'll be fine,' Jim said.

'Splendid. I will get Lee Fong to brush down your clothes while you relax.'

'I don't want to put anybody to any trouble.'

'No trouble, I assure you.' Van Otis turned to the waiting Chinaman. 'Lee Fong, will you show Mr McKendry the way to the bathroom?'

Lee Fong waved a slim hand, bowing slightly. 'You come, McKendly.'

Jim was feeling replete. The meal had been superb. Now van Otis and he were in the big room, sitting in armchairs each side of a huge log fire crackling in the vast grate. Van Otis was smoking a fine cigar and occasionally sipping a very fine French brandy out of a glass made for the experience. Jim was doing the same. It was liquor he had not tasted before. Unlike the rotgut he was used to, he found this drink smooth and silky on his palate, warm in his stomach. He decided he could easily get used to such an exquisite flavour.

After savouring the brandy he said, 'I can think of worse ways to spend an evening.'

Van Otis smiled. 'Yes, I suppose life on the ranch can be a little basic.'

'Not when you are brought up to it.'

'Of course.' Van Otis swirled the brandy around the bottom of his glass. 'Now, Mr McKendry, what is the purpose of your visit? Do you have news regarding the killer of my mother and your father?'

'No. I want to know what you were doing in Flat Rock?'

Van Otis looked surprised. He said, 'Why, I thought I told you . . . business, and yet another attempt to try and find the man who killed my mother.'

'You were awful sure he would be there.'

'I was and what is more I have been proved right.'

Jim narrowed his eyelids. 'What do you mean?'

Van Otis looked puzzled and then he said, 'Oh, dear, you obviously haven't heard.'

'Heard what?'

'There has been another killing. Your brother . . . by adoption? Callum, is it? Found murdered in the usual horrible way?'

Jim nodded. 'Oh! I've heard all right. That is why I am here. I figure you killed him. I think that was the real reason why you were in Flat Rock.'

Van Otis leaned up off the back of his chair to

stare at him with amazed black eyes. He said, '*Me?* Why, you must be mad. Dammit, sir, I find your accusation grossly insulting.'

'You do, huh?'

'Yes, I do.'

Van Otis slowly settled back in his chair, clearly still annoyed. He said, 'Really, Mr McKendry, you most certainly would have spoiled my meal had we talked about this over dinner. It is totally absurd. How on earth did you arrive at such a ridiculous deduction?'

Jim said, 'I'm coming round to that. But just now I'm curious as to why you took so long to get back here? Henry Baron, the stable owner at Flat Rock, said you picked up your horse around ten o'clock at night four days ago.'

Van Otis's black eyes suddenly became pools of dark menace. He said quietly, 'I am beginning to find this whole thing very distasteful, Mr McKendry. And, the idea of you spying on me is most disturbing.'

'It shouldn't be,' Jim said easily. 'Now, answer me this . . . why did it take you so long to get back to here?'

Van Otis was looking peevish and impatient now. He said, 'Really, this is beginning to get tedious and it saddens me. Apart from Lee Fong, I lead a solitary life out here, Mr McKendry. I have few guests to speak of. Nevertheless, for once I was looking forward to a pleasant evening by the fire talking about the ranching profession and the adventures you people undoubtedly have while executing that hazardous occupation.' Van Otis sighed as if he was bitterly disappointed. 'Mr McKendry, the reason why I was late arriving here is a very simple one. My horse went lame. I made a detour to the Bar D ranch on the Yellowstone in order to make a trade for a sound beast. I was invited to supper and to stay the night.'

Jim felt he was a balloon and was slowly deflating. 'The hell you were. Well, I guess I can check that out on the way back to Flat Rock.'

Van Otis got up. He was clearly very angry. 'Really, sir! You have ruined the entire evening. I bid you goodnight.' He made a step or two and then paused and turned. 'But, still in the tradition of the West, I will not deny you refuge, nor breakfast in the morning. Even so, I expect you to be off my premises immediately afterwards. Do we have an understanding?'

'Couldn't have put it plainer myself,' Jim said. But thought: I'm not finished with you yet, mister. However he added, 'Sweet dreams.'

Van Otis stared. 'Pardon me if I do not reciprocate. You have spoiled my entire evening.'

CHAPTER TWENTY

The big clock in the large hall chimed two as Jim passed it. Its ringing tones startled him, for the whole vast house was cathedral silent. When he entered the big lounge it, too, was quiet. Only the logs in the huge grate occasionally popped and crackled. Fortunately, as well as heat, the fire threw out enough light to enable him to find the diaries he saw earlier, lined up on the bookshelves. With considerable anticipation, he took them down, crossed to the plush chair near the fire. He opened the first volume.

The diaries of Christian van Otis, Volume One.

What he read amazed him. The first entry was dated 10 June 1869:

This day Marian van Otis met her end peacefully and by my hand. I could not allow her to return to Holland, dragging me with her. But I do consider she is now in a better place. Sic transit gloria mundi*.

* So passes away earthly glory.

Jim did not understand the last part. It was in a foreign language, but, hell, the rest of it was plain enough. Van Otis had killed his mother! Feverishly, he grabbed the third volume. He opened it at the end. The entry before the last one read:

John McKendry eliminated on the instructions of Callum Bowden: one thousand dollars.

The last entry was the mine owner's death in Elk Butte.

God Almighty!

The voice from behind sent thrills of nerves surging through Jim. 'Do they make interesting reading, Mr McKendry?'

Knowing the knifeman liked to slit throats Jim leapt forward out of the chair and then swung around to face him. Van Otis was close to the back of the chair, grinning his death's-head grin, his knife poised.

'Interesting isn't the word,' Jim said, trying to control the stroke of his heart, which was now thumping violently against his ribs. He clawed at his right hip for his six-gun and found it wasn't there. He was in his red long johns and the dressing gown that had been laid out for him on the bed when he went up to retire.

Jesus!

'Oh, dear,' van Otis was saying, 'no weapon, Jim?'

McKendry quickly calmed down. But still, cold anger lay seething in the pit of his stomach. With a cold grey stare he studied van Otis's pale face, the slim blade in his hand, which glinted orange-red in the fire glow.

He said, 'Is that the knife you used to kill my father?'

Van Otis smiled and raised black brows. 'Why, yes; and on Callum, too, of course, as well as many more. You see, Jim – you don't mind if I call you Jim? – when I gave Mother eternal rest I found the elimination of the human species' – van Otis smirked – 'of which unfortunately I am a member, was an intensely invigorating and powerful experience. It made me feel like a God – omnipotent, superior. So much so I could not get enough of it. So I soon devised what I thought was the most efficient and indeed practical way to do my work. Guns are noisy; don't you think? Knives are quiet and just as lethal when used knowledgably.'

'You're sick,' Jim said, not hiding his loathing.

Van Otis lifted his black brows as if he was entering upon a debate. 'Odd as it may seem, at first, I thought the same. Then I realized I was giving a service, that what sickness there was lay with the people who instructed me to do their killing for them. Logical, don't you think?'

'Real sick,' Jim said. 'Who paid you to murder Callum?'

Van Otis smiled and looked as though he was surprised. 'Why, your sister, Betty Lou, and *eliminate* is a more acceptable word, don't you think? Murder, I find, is so . . . *emotive.*'

Jim stared, aghast. '*Betty Lou?*'

Jim felt an icy chill hit the pit of his stomach. What in God's name had driven her to do that?

Van Otis answered the question for him, tapping his chin thoughtfully, carrying on as though he liked the sound of his own voice, or was giving a ruminative lecture. 'Yes, I think Callum made the mistake of telling her what his full ambitions were. He also told me, yokel that he was. His ambitions were to own the Rafter M. Did you know that, Jim? No, of course you didn't. And to do it, having already got me to eliminate your father, he would need me first to kill you and then probably your mother. I can only assume Callum felt Betty Lou's love for him was strong enough to accept that appalling scenario. Clearly, it wasn't.' Van Otis smiled. 'But how admirable of the dear lady to want such a revenge. But the really sad part of it is I had to kill *her*, too, when she refused to pay me and tried to kill me for carrying out her orders!'

Jim let the astonishing news sink in. Callum ordered Pa's killing? And he had told sweet, gentle Betty Lou he had? No wonder she had appeared to be so anxious lately, so distracted, so fraught, carrying that sort of burden on her shoulders and being told such a thing by the son of a bitch she loved to distraction.

He said, 'You're something else, van Otis; d'you know that?'

Van Otis smiled. 'Yes, I am rather special, aren't I?' he said. 'But not in the way you mean, Jim. I am not a demon. I dispose of people's worries. I am the tool they use to fulfil their murderous intent.'

Jim said, 'Mister, I'm going to send you to hell, you hear me?'

Van smiled his tombstone smile. 'And how, prey, are you going to do that, Jim? You are unarmed and I have Lee Fong behind you just in case you are lucky enough to get past *me*.'

Fighting force flared through Jim, tingling like a spray of hot iron filings through his racing blood. He swung around – swift, lithe and slick as a cougar.

Lee Fong, he saw, despite his disabilities, was moving as fast as he could towards him, yelling, a butcher's cleaver lifted menacingly above his head. Jim let him come on and then he stepped briskly aside.

The lethal blade swept past his right shoulder, slicing open the flannel material and grazing off skin. The instant pain from the wound burnt like fire through him. But Lee Fong was unbalanced. He was staggering forward, obviously hindered by his incapacities. Jim took full advantage. He kicked the Chinaman in the kidneys as he went past. Lee Fong screamed his pain. Jim followed up with another powerful strike, hitting Lee Fong with an iron-hard fist in the temple. Lee Fong went groggy and sank to his knees, dropping the cleaver on the way down. Jim ran forward and picked up the hatchet.

He turned to see, in the flickering light of the fire, van Otis advancing, thin gutting knife clenched in his hand. There was a manic light in his eyes; he

155

looked delighted with the situation and clearly lusting for blood.

Jim said, 'This won't be as easy as the others, van Otis.'

Van Otis sneered a smile. 'Ha! A man with similar confidence to my own; I like that.'

He flicked the knife, suddenly, unexpectedly. It flashed red in the firelight as it sped across the room. But Jim was intensely focused. He parried the blade with the cleaver. The clash of steel against steel rang out across the stillness of the big room. The deflected knife hit the wall to Jim's left and clattered to the floor. Jim did not heed it. Van Otis was coming at him with another blade, which he had obviously tucked into a pocket of his silk dressing gown, just in case.

Jim reacted, again with precision. He hefted the weight of the cleaver in his hand. He calculated what would be needed to make the blade fly true, and then he threw it with all the force he could muster. The cleaver hit van Otis full in the face, splitting his nose and crashing through the front of his skull – the speed at which it was travelling causing it to enter the brain.

Van Otis did not die immediately, or fall down. He began tottering about as if he was drunk, screaming and clawing at the cleaver. Jim ran forward and pulled at the blade. It did not release immediately and he was dragging van Otis around the room with him. When it did pull free, Jim really did make a job of killing the evil son of a bitch: one blow that split his skull wide open.

But now Jim realized Lee Fong was on his back, clinging like a leech, squeezing his throat with a power that did not seem possible in so small and so crippled a man. Jim back-pedalled as fast as he could. He smashed Lee Fong with brute force into the oak panels of the wall behind them.

He heard bones crunch under the impact. Lee Fong cried out and his grip relaxed a little. Jim smashed him once, twice, three times more against the solid panels, using his powerful legs for leverage, his back as a ram.

Lee Fong shrieked with each blow before he fell to the ground to lie moaning on the deep pile carpet of the grand room. Blood was running freely from his mouth. Jim assumed there must be bad internal injuries. He looked down without sympathy and said, 'It hurts, uh?'

He collected van Otis's knives and the cleaver in case Lee Fong was not as badly hurt as he appeared to be. He went back upstairs, got dressed and strapped on his Colt .45. He returned to the huge lounge. He found all was tomb quiet. Large pools of blood surrounded both bodies.

Jim bent and felt the big vein in Lee Fong's neck. It was still. There was no sign of life in the man. In the silence the fire spat and crackled, casting flickering light on to the rich furnishings and the rows of bound books. Jim stared at them and then said quietly, 'I guess that wraps it up, Pa.'

He picked up the three diaries, left the room, went

through the front door, closing it behind him. He paced over to the stables, his shadow dark and long in the silver light of the half moon hanging in the star-filled night sky behind him.

Ten minutes later he was riding out, taking the trail to Elk Butte.

EPILOGUE

After Jim got the doctor in Elk Butte to fix his grazed shoulder he went over to the marshal's office. Silently, Marshal Rimmer read the parts of the diaries that mattered, glancing up occasionally, looking uncomfortable and shaking his head. After a few minutes he said, 'Van Otis of all people; fifty-six entries . . . deaths, *eliminations* as he calls them. It don't bear thinking about.'

Jim said, 'It's all there, nevertheless.'

'Yeah.' Rimmer's stare turned quizzical. 'And no mention at all who paid to have Callum Bowden killed?'

'No,' said Jim. 'Seems he never got around to entering that. Reckon, now, we'll never know.'

'Pity,' Rimmer said.

Not in my book, thought Jim. That was his business and would remain so. Betty Lou had rid the world of a first-class skunk. Her memory was to be cherished. Ma and he would grieve together and remember together and hold Betty Lou's courage for

159

ever in their hearts.

They rode to the grand van Otis house. They took three deputies with them. Rimmer accepted Jim's account of how van Otis and Lee Fong died and exonerated him of all blame. The sons of bitches deserved all they got, was Rimmer's heartfelt opinion. Then they buried the dead, not too reverently, and returned to Elk Butte.

Next morning Jim hit the trail for Flat Rock. But the story did not end there. Six months later Jim led the lovely Lisette Simon down the aisle of Flat Rock's one and only church. To most everybody's surprise she took to ranch life and marriage like she took to everything else . . . wholeheartedly.

The ranch prospered, Jim using his cow-nous, Lisette using her business know-how. The five children the union produced all grew up to be their pride and joy and pillars of Montana society. So did their numerous grandchildren and great grandchildren. Not bad, for a numb-head cowpuncher and the most beautiful woman in the world.